# BETRAYED

**Kavita Daswani** is an international journalist covering fashion, beauty, travel, design and celebrities for a range of global publications. A former fashion editor for the *South China Morning Post* in Hong Kong and Asian correspondent for *WWD*, for whom she still writes, she currently contributes to the *Los Angeles Times*, *Cosmetic News Weekly*, *Tatler*, *Crave* and numerous other publications.

She has also written for the Indian editions of *Vogue*, *Conde Nast Traveller* and *Grazia Italia*.

She lives in Los Angeles with her husband and two sons. She has authored the best-selling books *For Matrimonial Purposes*, *The Village Bride of Beverly Hills*, *Indie Girl*, *Salaam, Paris* and *Bombay Girl*. Her books have been published in seventeen languages.

# BETRAYED

*Kavita Daswani*

HarperCollins *Publishers* India

First published in India in 2014 by
HarperCollins *Publishers* India
Building 10, Tower A, 4th Floor, DLF Cyber City, Phase II,
Gurugram Haryana – 122002, India
www.harpercollins.co.in



P-ISBN: 978-93-5136-374-3
E-ISBN: 978-93-5136-375-0

2 4 6 8 10 9 7 5 3 1



Typeset in ITC Giovanni Std 10.5/14
By Saanvi Graphics Noida

Printed and bound at
MicroPrints India, New Delhi

*To my husband, my one and only, always.*

# PROLOGUE

The zipper on my dress caught. I arched my back, threw my right arm over my shoulder and strained as I fiddled with it. It stuck stubbornly, attached to a lacy fragment of the scarlet-red Valentino cocktail dress I had bought for tonight.

'Chanoo!' I called out through my half-open door. Our gray-haired helper, the head of our coterie of staff and the woman who had tended to me since I was born, raced in. I turned around, indicated the problem and left her to her devices. Chanoo knew how to fix anything. She steadied herself – as would a surgeon going in for a triple bypass – flattened the dress against my spine and went to work, breathing audibly through her nose.

I didn't need this wardrobe malfunction right now. I had bought the dress in Hong Kong recently, on a shopping excursion with my mother. She had said I could have anything for tonight. I had chosen this, a crepe and Chantilly lace confection that fit me perfectly. I had been immediately drawn to the vibrancy of it; a red that signaled celebration, a dress designed to make an impact.

I felt the zipper closing up, snugly. Chanoo patted it down, rewarding it for finally behaving. I turned to one side and looked at myself in the full-length mirror. The liquid diet I'd been on for two weeks had worked; my stomach was actually concave. I was glad I'd disregarded my dietician's theories that tomato soup, double espressos and vodka do not a healthy diet make. The pounds had melted off, even though I realized they would pile back on the second I consumed one of Chanoo's famous aloo parathas. The Victoria's Secret push-up bra was doing a terrific job; my cleavage now approached my chin. Simple solitaires gleamed in my ears and on my feet were sky-high, gold Louboutins, whose soles matched my dress. I spritzed on some custom-made perfume, picked up my metallic snakeskin clutch and made ready to go.

I was going to stun my family tonight. And not just because of how I looked.

Martin Veitch, my new partner – the man who would be sharing the spotlight with me this evening – should have landed five hours ago and would be arriving at the party around the same time that I would. I had specifically booked a room for him at the InterContinental, facing Marine Drive. As a California man, he would appreciate the sea view. He would have more than enough time for a shower and maybe even a quick nap before it was time to meet me in Dome, where the party was happening, the party that warranted a red dress from Valentino.

In the elevator, on the way down to the car, my parents stood on either side of me. My father looked at me, frowning, his expression bordering on anxious.

'What?' I asked him.

'It seems you have gone to a lot of trouble and expense for tonight,' he said. 'Maybe we could have arranged something more private and simple?'

I didn't reply as I watched the numbers light up as we descended, feeling mildly annoyed. Trust my father to try and squash my enthusiasm.

'I'm just saying, Beta, that if you are only presenting a business idea to Baba, then there's no need for a fancy cocktail party. Is there?'

'Please, Dad, just let me do things my way,' I said, setting my jaw defiantly, thereby terminating the conversation.

I could not, however, dispute my father's opinion. Yes, tonight's guests were pretty much family, with just a few key outsiders. I was making a proposal to Baba. But the proposal was so carefully thought out, so meticulously researched and planned, that I felt entirely justified in planning a party. This needed to be more than just a standard presentation. This had to be an event.

It should have only taken fifteen minutes to get from Neapean Sea Road to Churchgate, but it was Saturday night and the drive took three times as long. Still, there was no reason to worry; my relatives would arrive, mingle, have a cocktail. Then, Martin and I would make our entrance and our announcement. Nitya, my best friend, would be there too, as well as my cousin Milan's girlfriend, Anushka, who had pledged her support for my endeavours from the beginning. I checked my phone only to feel yet another layer of excitement; Bharat had texted to say he was getting ready and would see me there. Tonight, he'd be officially meeting my family for the first time and I wondered what they would think of him, if their opinions would help clarify my own feelings for him.

Finally, we pulled up at the hotel. My mother and I glided up to the reception desk.

'Can you call Mr Veitch and tell him that Sohana Badshah is here?' I asked the clerk. He consulted his computer.

'Ma'am, the guest has not yet checked in,' he said.

'Oh,' I replied. I looked at my watch and frowned. The traffic can't have been that bad, even on a Saturday, even in Bombay.

'Maybe his flight was delayed, Ma'am,' the clerk said. 'Would you like me to check for you?'

'Please do,' I said. Martin had had some meetings in Dubai. I'd sent him a First Class ticket, even though my father had said that Business was more than adequate. But I wanted to go the extra mile. He would have been the first one off the plane. He would have breezed right through. He should have been here by now. He'd said he'd text me as soon as he landed, but I hadn't heard from him since he had left his home in Los Angeles for Dubai four days ago.

The front desk clerk hung up the phone and turned his attention back to me. 'Ma'am, the flight landed on time.'

I nodded, puzzled.

'What's the problem?' my father asked, appearing behind me.

'Martin's not here yet,' I said.

'Must have been some hold-up,' said my father. 'I have spent two hours just getting out of the goddamn Arrivals area. That bloody airport is useless.'

'Dad, please,' I said. 'Not now.' My father loved complaining about the chaos at the airport.

'Don't worry, Beta,' my mother soothed. 'He must be on his way. Come. Let's go up. Everything will be okay.'

I walked into Dome, the gorgeous rooftop bar, and Anushka was the first to come up to me, smiling in her dazzling, inimitable way. She was becoming an increasingly sought-after actress, now making the transition from stage to silver screen, and I was honoured she had taken the time to show up. Milan, though, was nowhere to be seen.

Anushka squeezed my hand. 'This is so exciting!' she said. 'Thank you for inviting me!'

She was by far, the best girlfriend that Milan had ever had, and there had been plenty. I had told him, shortly after they had started going out, that she was someone to hang on to, that in addition to being lovely to look at, she had a kind heart – a rare thing in these circles. She was the sort of girl anyone would want their brother to marry. And even if Milan wasn't my real brother, he felt like one – at least he used to, when things were smooth between us, and hopefully would again soon. I wanted him to be happy.

'Is Milan coming?' I asked her.

She shrugged. 'He's having a little trouble with all this,' she said.

I looked across at the candlelit space and stood still for a second, letting the cool December breeze settle over me. It was a large space, probably too big for a private family party. But, as I'd told my father, I wanted to present my idea against this elegant, sophisticated backdrop. I wanted to make an impression on Baba, on Mr Veitch, on all of them. I loved this hotel. Milan and I were regular patrons of the InterContinental. This was where I entertained my out-of-town guests, it was the place Nitya and I chose for all our inane celebrations. It made sense that I would have my coming-out party here. At the grand age of twenty-seven, I was finally making my bid to stand up and be counted.

On a white couch at the furthest end, I spotted Baba and Dadi, my grandparents, the centre of their own universe, waiters drifting around them, my grandfather showing scant interest in anyone, my grandmother being gracious.

Pawan, Milan's twin brother, stood alone, holding a glass of tomato juice. He raised a hand in my direction, waving very deliberately, his fingers following the pattern of a slow-motion wave. He was the plainest of all the Badshah boys, a loner, almost always awkward, especially now, compared to our more glamorous relatives. I looked for my older brother, Armaan, who was flying home from Warsaw tonight, and had said he would be coming straight here. He hadn't arrived yet. Whether he made it here or not, I knew Ekta, his girlfriend and 'intended', would not be accompanying him. Baba had expressly instructed Armaan not to go public about his relationship with 'India's top supermodel', as she was widely known, until he was ready to give his blessing. Baba had not quite approved of the match, writing Ekta off as too forward, too avant-garde in her lifestyle, too lax in her morals. The only reason Anushka was here was because Milan had not yet introduced her to our grandparents, which, given Baba's reluctance to allow just anyone into the fold, was probably a smart move. As far as everyone here tonight was concerned,

Anushka was just another one of my friends, present to lend her support. Out of the corner of my eye, I saw my aunt, Malini, in conversation with my mother, clutching a glass of Bordeaux, the size of a birdbath. Her husband, Amit Uncle, stood alone by the bar, staring at Malini with a look vaguely approximating contempt; their marriage had been under duress for a while now, since rumours had begun to surface that Malini was having an affair with a famous cricket player.

'Hello sweetheart,' I heard behind me. Preeti, my chachi, and by far my favoured one, stood behind me in a beautiful cobalt blue jersey dress that drooped sexily in the back. She was Milan's and Pawan's mother but could easily have passed for an elder sister.

'You are beautiful tonight, Sohana,' she said. 'Love the red on you.'

'Has everyone else arrived?' I asked her. I should have been more concerned that the guest of honour, my new partner, the reason we were all even here tonight, had not.

'Jaanvi,' she said, indicating my cousin-in-law, the wife of my oldest cousin Sharan. 'And, of course, Jeetu,' she said brightly, pointing out her husband, who had joined my father. 'Anyway, my darling, the people who are meant to be here, are. This is your night.'

I stared in front of me. A podium had been set up – a lectern, two microphones, side by side, coupled. Overhead, there was a big screen, a laptop off to one side, bespectacled tech whizzes to run the whole thing. Everything was in place. All I needed was Martin. And he wasn't here.

Raghu, my dad's personal assistant and someone I had come to 'borrow' more often lately, approached me, clutching his iPad. 'Ma'am, the family is waiting,' he said.

'Just give Mr Veitch a few more minutes,' I replied glancing towards the entrance. 'Any updates?'

Raghu scurried off, tapping numbers on his mobile and I returned to socializing, my mind distracted. A few minutes later, he returned.

'Ma'am, it seems that the driver never picked him up,' he said, matter-of-factly. 'He waited and waited. Mr Veitch did not show himself.'

I frowned, confused. I didn't handle this sort of thing well – when things that shouldn't happen did. I'd never been any good at it.

'Well, then the driver simply didn't see him,' I said loudly. I was aware that I was scolding Raghu. 'Mr Veitch is probably making his own way.'

'Yes, Ma'am.' Raghu said.

'He will get here,' I said.

'Yes, Ma'am,' he parroted, irritatingly.

My mother came over, put her hand on my arm. 'Baba's getting impatient, Beta,' she said. 'So just start, okay?'

Nitya stood behind me, holding my purse after I fished out small cards with my hand-written notes. As I turned, I saw Milan walk in and go straight to Anushka's side, leaving enough room between them, so as not to raise any eyebrows. I was heartened that he had come. Now, I just needed to see Martin. And Bharat.

But Baba was twitching impatiently, looking grumpier than usual and I knew I that I had to suddenly and spontaneously reconfigure this. The whole evening had been planned perfectly with Martin over nightly Google Hangout sessions. I was to have gone up first, introduced him and he would have taken over and done the bulk of the speaking, answered questions and pointed out, on the screen behind him, with the deft aid of the audio-visual team, the car. The Car. The Vecco. It was going to change his life and mine. And the course of Badshah Industries, my grandfather's empire.

But he wasn't here. And as I'd learnt from endless screenings of 'Celebrity Apprentice', which had annoyed me as much as enlightened me, I had to 'step up'. This was a classic 'What Would Trump Do?' moment.

I swallowed a shot of tequila handed to me by Nitya, who had taught me that a little alcohol can go a long way in making things right. She put her hand on the small of my back, just as she had done months earlier, the night all this had started and pushed me forward.

'Go,' she said. 'It's just your family. Go.'

I saw my great uncle, Matunga Dada, walk in and go straight to Preeti. I nearly cried. I wanted to run over and hug him, have him take away the sickness in my belly. He stood gazing at me, his hands behind his back, wearing an ill-fitting black suit. The sleeves of the jacket stopped short of his wrists and it clung to him, far too tightly, around his chest. It would smell of mothballs. I recognized the suit from four years ago, on the occasion of my cousin Sharan's marriage to Jaanvi; it would have been the last time he would have worn it. Now, his eyes didn't leave me. His face was placid, loving, assured – the same expression he always wore every time he looked at me.

I approached the lectern.

'Good evening everyone,' I said into the

microphone. There was a momentary screech before the tech-whizzes fiddled and fixed it. For a moment, the ridiculousness of what I was doing settled on me. I was putting forth a serious business idea directly to my grandfather, clad in a red lace dress. Perhaps there might have been a more sensible approach. But, as I looked at the expectant faces in front of me, it was a little late in the day for a change of heart.

'Thank you all so much for coming here tonight,' I said. I was sick with nerves. 'I invited you all here this evening to announce some plans.' I paused. 'The idea was to make this announcement with my partner, Mr Martin Veitch, from Los Angeles. But it seems he has been unavoidably detained. He is still at the Mumbai airport. Perhaps he will make it here by Christmas.' I smiled. A titter went through my guests like a fissure in the ice. Everyone had tales about the airport.

I took a deep breath.

On the screen behind me, beneath the large, spotlit Badshah Industries logo, appeared an image of a shiny white car.

'Baba,' I said, directing my gaze straight at my grandfather, for whom this whole production had been orchestrated. 'This is the Vecco. It is entirely hydro-powered; the first of its kind. We have already made the investment. The Vecco can be in production within eighteen months. We have a manufacturing plant set up in Gujarat. We anticipate a strong national demand.' I tried to remember what Martin had planned on saying. 'The Vecco is a symbol of all that is new about Badshah Industries, a company that has always been on the cutting edge.'

Once I started getting the words out, I felt my body relax. It was remarkably quiet on that rooftop; I could hear little more than the sound of ice cubes tinkling in glasses. It was a beautiful night in my city; the air felt bracing, the moon was high – a person could almost feel invincible.

'With the investment from Badshah Industries, we can slowly start getting people off their addiction to oil,' I said proudly. 'We anticipate this to be the way forward, not just for Badshah, but for all of India.'

I had figures prepared; average household petrol consumption, how many more cars were expected to travel on India's roads between now and 2020 – these were statistics that a consultancy firm I had hired, at Martin's suggestion, had researched for me. I started to recite them, my confidence bolstered with every word, every compelling number.

But I didn't get a chance to finish. Raghu startled me from behind. 'Miss Badshah,' he said, leaning his head towards mine, his tone suddenly less deferential. 'You have to end this. There is a problem.'

# PART ONE

# ONE

Eight Months Ago.

It was noisy outside Privee. But Jag, my former boyfriend, the man I loved, could hear me perfectly.

'Talk to me,' he said, gently.

'I need to do this,' I said. I was breathing heavily, Nitya standing next to me protectively. My phone was pressed up against my ear and I blanked out everything happening around me – the people beckoning me to go back into the nightclub, telling me they'd call so we'd get together.

'What's going on?' Jag asked

'I want to take over the business.'

'Okay,' he said simply. 'Let's figure this out.'

We talked a few minutes more. When I put my phone away, there were tears in my eyes. Nitya led me out of the fray to my waiting car. 'Deep breath,' she said, mimicking one of the lithe teachers that ran the chain of yoga studios she had just sold for a sum even she conceded was far more than they were worth. We had been out celebrating.

Inside Privee earlier, as the world danced around us, I had made a decision. While girls with phony smiles air-kissed and boys strutted like peacocks, clad in D&G, I made the sudden, ill-conceived decision to fight for control of my grandfather's company. And Jag, the man I had once hoped I would wed, was the first person I called, validating just how much I still loved him, no matter how hard I tried to deny it.

Now, my chauffeur, Rohit, opened the door and I stepped into the cool air-conditioned quiet, Nitya's hand still on my arm. Rohit started the engine, asking where I wanted to go next. I stared out of the window as we pulled out onto the dark, pockmarked road. It was almost one in the morning. In my former life, Privee would have been among several stops of an evening out. But not tonight.

'What am I going to do?' I asked Nitya. The significance and utter absurdity of my intentions, settled on me. I, Sohana Badshah, generally useless heiress, a Bombay Girl in the much-maligned monied category, had decided to make a bid to take over a business conglomerate that I knew almost nothing about. Had I really had that much champagne in there?

'Don't worry about that,' said Nitya, settling into the seat. 'Right now, we go home.'

That night, I dreamt about a little girl on a garden path. She was in a gauzy white dress. She treaded carefully down a pristine marble hallway that felt cement-cold on her bare feet, but had been polished with gold. She stopped at a massive engraved door, outside which sat a forlorn dholi.

The little girl turned around to look at the path that she had just come down and saw that it had morphed into something else – crooked, overgrown with thorns, meandering off into nowhere. The door had vanished along with the dholi. As she headed off into the morass, the dream startled me awake.

Later that morning, I sat alone in the verandah, drinking tea and eating freshly-buttered toast, waiting for my parents to join me. I had gone to bed feeling sick to my stomach; I had made a powerful decision and the only people I had told were an old beau and my best friend.

Waking up that morning, I had felt hazy, disconnected. Nonsensical dreams notwithstanding, I could take it all back, disavow my interest in the family empire, let the boys fight over it, like they were supposed to. Nitya wouldn't hold it against me. Jag might – but should I really care about what he thought anymore?

Adding to my general sense of malaise was the fact that, in a few hours, I was supposed to meet with Manjuli Khosla, a business journalist who had been doggedly pursuing a story about my grandfather's plans for Badshah Industries. Word had leaked out in this compressed, incestuous town where gossip was a favourite pastime – second only to philandering – that my grandfather had had huge reservations about bequeathing his beloved company to his sons, that he was putting Badshah Industries on the market.

I would always see Manjuli as the person who had set all this in motion, who had, in my estimation of things, triggered the turbulence that had befallen my family. She was the one who had unearthed financial details about my family that few outside it had been privy to. She had written a startling newspaper exposé about the empire started by the secretive Darshan Badshah, my grandfather, and had gone on to publicly surmise that he now sat atop the wealthiest family-owned company in the nation. After that, Baba had revealed privately to the family that none of his three sons would be inheriting the business. He had made this declaration without providing a reason, for his sons – even the seemingly brash ones – had always unquestioningly deferred to his every judgement. Baba had only told us that if one of the grandchildren – namely one of the young men of the third-generation Badshah litter – didn't step forth and come up with a grandiose, yet eminently workable, plan to take Badshah to the next level, he would sell off the whole thing, lock, stock and brand new Bentley. We would never be poor, he assured us. There would be 'enough money for seven generations.' But we would be nothing more than heirs and heiresses, wealthy by virtue of the circumstances of our birth.

Baba's decision had unsettled and provoked us all, estranging cousins and brothers. Worse still, Manjuli Khosla clearly knew some of this, or certainly enough to threaten disclosure unless I gave her the scoop she had been hankering for. She had pestered me for weeks and I had finally relented, agreeing to meet her for coffee this morning.

Now, sitting with my parents, I skimmed the malai off the top of my tea and rounded it over the rim of the fine, porcelain cup in my hands. I was distracting myself, not wanting to settle on what was really gnawing away at me here – that I had no idea how my parents would react to what I was about to tell them, and that I couldn't predict how I would counter whatever their reaction might be. It would be stupidly idealistic of me, I realized, to think they'd leap with joy when I told them that I, the only granddaughter of the illustrious Badshah family and someone whose most notable accomplishment to date was a three-month stint at an interior design college in London, was going to make an attempt in good faith to take over a complex and fractured business.

More likely, they would dissuade me – as well they should. They would tell me all the ways it couldn't be done, why it shouldn't be done. That it was a man's game and I needed to leave it alone. And really, they would say, shouldn't I focus more on meaningful tasks, like trying to find a husband? They would say all this, and more. They would tell me I was jeopardizing my brother Armaan's stab at greatness, that my true role would be to help him – not set up shop across the street from him. And in none of this would they be wrong.

My father came in first, concluding a phone conversation. My mother trailed behind him. I stood up to greet them as if I were at a formal cocktail party at which the guests of honour had just arrived.

'Going somewhere?' my dad asked.

'Oh. No.'

'Then why are you standing?' He pressed a buzzer on the wall to summon one of the kitchen staff, gave instructions that his morning toast be replaced with papaya and prune juice, muttering to my mother about being mildly constipated lately. She put on her glasses, scanned the newspaper, clipped out an ad for an Ayurvedic doctor in Sion who claimed to be able to treat premature graying of hair, something that my mother was plagued by, even though, at fifty-five, it was hardly premature.

I leaned back in my chair and looked at them. This was it, really. This was an ordinary day in the lives of a supposedly extraordinary family – a mother anxious about losing her youthful looks, a father concerned about sluggish bowel movements. Their vast wealth notwithstanding, in some ways, they really were no different from any post-middle-aged couple in India.

'I'm going to try and take over the company,' I blurted out.

My father took a sip of tea and stared at me. For a second, the words drooped in the air between us. His face soured.

'This is not sweet enough,' he said. 'Chanoo!' he cried out. His morning voice had a guttural quality to it. Chanoo came in, holding a bowl of sugar, having anticipated my father's every need.

'Did you say something, Beta?' my mother now asked, delayed reaction kicking in. 'Very interesting article here about cayenne pepper preventing cancer.' She found her scissors and started clipping again.

'Actually, yes,' I said, more forcefully this time. I stood up, as if about to answer a question at school. A pile of newspapers slid from my lap to the floor. 'I have decided that I, too, would like to try and win the business.' There was a flutter in my voice.

My father stared at me. A big grin splayed across his face. 'Very cute,' he said, chuckling. 'Yes, Beta, why not?' He shook out the folds of the newspaper gently and resumed reading.

A hot flush went through my body. I sat down again. Of course, there was no reason they should take me seriously. The last time I had professed an unwavering commitment to anything was when I insisted I wanted to become an interior designer. They had sent me to London and I had dumped the course after twelve weeks, coming home to recoup from a broken relationship I never told them about. Before that, I had convinced my dad to give me money to invest in a friend's fashion line, which halted production two months later because she went off and got married. My father never asked me what became of it, assuming – quite rightly – that it was a lost cause. Then, after my brief, but successful, stint at learning how to cook, I'd even, just for a moment, considered opening a restaurant, but when I saw how much paperwork was involved, the volumes of red tape I'd have to circumvent, how many officials I'd have to pay off, I decided that I just didn't have the stomach for it after all.

So now, here I was, having never really proven myself, asking my parents to legitimately back me in a race for their legacy. Our legacy. Of course they weren't going to take me seriously.

My father stood up and stretched. He was going to play golf at Aamby Valley, with an assortment of other tycoons of varying pedigree. He'd be gone most of the day. I remained seated, toying mindlessly with the sash of my dressing gown. My mother folded her newspaper and came to sit in the chair next to me.

'Were you joking?' she asked.

I shook my head. She gazed at me with a look approximating love or pity – I couldn't quite tell.

'Okay,' she said.

'So?' I asked her. 'Now what?'

'Okay,' she repeated, before gathering her things and leaving the balcony.

# TWO

It was an unseasonably hot day; the sun raged in a grimy sky as I sat in the back of the car, tapping my fingers nervously on the cool glass window. I was late getting to the Kala Ghoda Café and traffic had stalled yet again. We had been waiting at one red light for eight minutes. Why people didn't just stay home in this heat was beyond me.

Maybe if I was really held up, Manjuli would leave. I texted her, told her I wasn't sure what time I would make it. She replied immediately – 'will wait.' My heart sank. My plan, the previous night, before I'd had my epiphany, had been to leave Privee early, head home and formulate a strategy for what I would tell Manjuli. All she wanted, of course, was the truth. But that was something I couldn't give her. But I couldn't lie to her either.

She had heard rumours about my grandfather courting outside interest in the business and I knew that that was what she wanted to talk to me about. She would ask me if it was true and she would probe to see if I knew anything else. Her editors had been harassing her for weeks for the story, and I had been her only real and credible source. She had done me a couple of favours, firstly by telling me what she knew about the lawsuit between my family and Jag's father – which had been the reason behind Jag leaving me – and secondly, she had agreed to withhold publishing any new information she might have until after she and I had spoken.

Now, it was time to make good on my promise to her. But I had to be smart about it. For a minute, I even considered switching agendas; I could keep my mouth shut on the business end of things and instead give her a real scoop – that the illustrious socialite, Malini Badshah, was sleeping with India's golden boy of cricket, Vivek Abbas. Then I realized that Manjuli Khosla was a business journalist and routinely pivoted away from the tawdrier aspects of Bombay high society.

We finally pulled up at the café. I paused outside the glass door and peered into the narrow, crowded white space. Manjuli was seated on a wooden bench, leaning against a wall. I pulled the door open and a burst of air conditioning hit me in the face. She stood up when she saw me, adjusted her dupatta and extended her hand to shake mine. In a minute, we were ordering macchiatos.

'Unfortunately, I don't have much time today,' I said. I wanted to let her know right up front that I wouldn't linger. Since we had arranged this meeting, everything had changed. I was now a participant in the race to win the Badshah company. I couldn't speak to her as an uninvolved bystander because I wasn't one. She pulled out a scrappy notebook and a pen which had clearly been chewed on. For someone who covered the biggest tycoons in India, she had a surprisingly nervous disposition.

'Before we start,' I said, 'I just want to thank you for holding off on publishing anything so far. I'm grateful.' What had Jag taught me? In negotiations, charm and disarm.

'That's okay,' she said. 'I took your word. And please, don't worry. Nothing can ever be traced back to you. You will be quoted only as a source.'

She picked up her pen, poised to scribble. 'Is it true that your grandfather is planning to sell Badshah Industries?' she asked.

'No.'

She looked up at me, sceptical. 'That's what reports in town say,' she said.

'Right now, he's not planning to sell the company,' I said. It was the truth.

She put her pen down, stared resolutely at me. 'Miss Badshah, I've been a business journalist for many years. I can tell when there is a story. There is something going on.'

I raised my fingers to my forehead and rubbed the patch between my eyebrows. I hated this. I shouldn't be talking about our private family business with an outsider. But I had made a promise and I knew she wouldn't allow me to go back on that now.

'Here it is,' I said, pushing my cup away and leaning forward. 'As of this moment, my grandfather has told the family privately that he will not allow any of his sons to inherit the business.'

Her eyes opened wide. 'Why?' she asked.

'That is not something I can answer,' I said. 'I do not know.'

'So if the business won't go to any of the sons, and he doesn't want to sell it to an outsider, what will become of Badshah?'

Two young women at the next table glanced our way. They looked like the sort who would read Page Three. They knew who I was. I lowered my voice and Manjuli strained to hear me. 'He has asked his grandsons to submit proposals,' I said.

'For?'

'Ideas. Something to take Badshah to the next level. Something revolutionary. He will bypass his sons and he will choose a successor among the grandsons.' I rued the words almost as soon as they tripped off my tongue. I knew it was wrong, traitorous even, telling her this. Baba, the intensely private person he was, didn't want anyone outside the family to know his plans. He expected to simply hand off the business to one of the grandsons and hope that nobody would notice. He didn't need it broadcasted in the pages of the leading daily newspaper in India. I knew what I was telling her would have dire repercussions, that it would leave my father and his brothers looking like dolts who were undeserving of even a cursory inheritance of a family business – something all sons could expect if they wanted it. In our circles, it was unheard of. In our circles, even complete morons inherited the family business.

Manjuli's mouth fell open. I scanned her face as she processed this new information about a decades-old, privately-held family company, long established in the firmament of the Indian business world, its members high-profile fixtures on the social circuit. Darshan Badshah was an elder statesman of the community. He may not have been beloved by everyone, but he was known, feared and admired.

'Oh,' she said. 'I've never heard of anything like this before. And I've been covering business for eleven years.'

'Yes. It was unexpected,' I said. The less I said now, the better. I'd answered enough of her questions. We were even.

'How will you put it,' I asked her, 'without making my dad and uncles look like failures?'

That had been at the heart of this the whole time. In Bollywood terms, it was some trollop of a starlet taking on a role destined for Rekha. Here was my grandfather, choosing to entrust his empire – five decades of work – to a twenty-something-year-old with an oversupply of testosterone, rather than to one of his more evolved, measured sons.

'Is he senile?' she asked.

'What?' I shouted, aghast.

'Alzheimer's? Dementia? Is there something wrong with your grandfather?'

'No! And please don't even imply that!'

She flipped over the cover of her notebook to shut it, slid her pen inside its wiry coils. 'The answer lies with your grandmother,' she said.

'What?'

'If you want to know why your grandfather is doing what he's doing, ask his wife. If anyone knows, she does.'

With that, she picked up her things and left. I sat there, dejected, and not just because I should have been the one to have made the dramatic exit.

# THREE

At home, I started thinking about who I could trust.

Now that the matter with Manjuli had been tended to, I realized that with my decision, I was potentially putting myself in the middle of a family firestorm. Still, I knew that truly smart people surrounded themselves with other smart people and that whatever I planned to do, I couldn't do it alone. I was going to need the right kind of support – people who wished me well and wanted me to succeed. I wasn't sure who in my family would qualify because so many of them were my competitors. In the eyes of Milan, my closest cousin, or my older brother, Armaan, I would be a traitor, trying to wrest from them the empire they were individually plotting to control. The fact that I stood to upset so many – me, a girl who aimed to please – made me really quite sick.

Later that afternoon, Nitya dropped in. She was still on a high from having sold her chain of yoga studios, something she had never expected to do. It had just about been breaking even, allowing Nitya to cover her overheads but certainly not to subsidize the life she envisioned for herself. So she had been taken aback when a boutique luxury hotel chain made an offer to buy it; it turned out that the hotelier's wife adored the hip and trendy vibe Nitya had endowed her business with, and the locations – Kemps Corner, Nariman Point, Bandra – had aligned perfectly with the hotel group's expansion plans. In that competitive market, they would be able to offer foreign visitors chauffeured services to adjacent, authentic Indian yoga experiences that would make them feel as though they were in Malibu or Manhattan. It was a win-win. And Nitya came away with much more than she ever bargained for.

'Look,' I said to her. 'Now that you've sold your company for all this money, don't you think you should pay your dad back what he invested in it?'

Nitya had managed to get her yoga studios off the ground through a sizable investment from her father. Like so many of us Bombay girls, she had dipped into somebody else's fortune – a father's, a husband's, a brother's, some sugar daddy's – to get her dream gig going. But, ironically, while Nitya's 'Om Sweet Om' yoga chain had had a happy ending, her father had made some poor business choices of his own. He had just barely started to re-establish himself. Repaying him from her substantial profits seemed like the right thing to do.

'Please,' she said, waving my suggestion away dismissively. 'As if my dad would even take it. He wants me to keep everything.'

'Sure he does,' I said, smiling. Oddly, I admired Nitya's cavalier attitude. It had always served her.

'I'm going to do something else with the proceeds,' she said. 'I could stop now, with one successful business under my belt. But I won't. I got lucky with Om Sweet Om. I think there's more.'

This was what we were all dealing with, Nitya and I, and girls like us. It was one thing to have an education, to be happy, to be 'settled', to have a career even. It was quite another to pound against that infernal glass ceiling. Nitya's father had thought it a good idea that his daughter wanted to set up a chain of yoga studios; he had said that it would 'keep her occupied'. Little had he known that it would become a bona fide brand with a vibe to call its own, that it would, before long, bring in a substantial offer.

Finally, Nitya had confided in me, her father had looked at the balance sheets and had conceded that, yes, his daughter had done well. If it had been Nitya's brother, there would have been back-slapping and boozing to celebrate, a multitude of shabaash's all round. Nitya, in her father's view, had simply been lucky. But Nitya took none of that to heart. She sold the business, banked the cash and her confidence exploded. She felt she could do anything.

Still, she knew exactly what I was up against with my own family; I had a compulsively domineering grandfather whose sole focus had been to control every aspect of the business. He mostly ignored his sons, but he encouraged his grandsons, provided they did as he expected. I knew he loved me, thought me pleasant and sweet, but that the one way I could really make him happy was to get married. Marry soon. Marry well. All else was secondary.

'Let's figure out what you're going to do,' she said. 'You don't have a lot of time, you know. Don't think for a second that your cousins are sitting around playing with themselves. They each want to be the first to show Baba something. I will guarantee you that while you are having useless meetings with journalists, those boys are getting work done.'

'I told my parents what I was planning and even they more or less ignored me.'

'Good,' she said, putting down her tea. 'That's the best way. They'll never see it coming.'

'So where do I start?' I said, grabbing my iPad.

'That trip you made to LA,' Nitya said, 'for Milan. There must be something in there that you can use.'

'I thought of that. But I was there for Milan. I don't feel right about pursuing any of those things on my own.'

'Oh, please!' protested Nitya. 'You're going to let some loyalty to your idiot cousin get in the way of what you need to do?'

'He's not an idiot,' I said, quietly.

'He is if he thinks that you will be nothing more than his errand girl,' she said. 'Go back, look at what you discovered for him. If he's not doing anything with it, it's fair game. You say you want to take over your grandfather's company? Then, bloody hell, do something. Be ruthless, if you have to. You want to play with the men? Then you have to act like a man.'

I did love Nitya – she was bold, loyal, forthright. But I was grateful when she finally left; I needed time to think.

Actually, what I needed to do was talk to Milan and Armaan. I wanted to not be afraid of their reaction to my decision. They might not approve, but, surely, they would have to respect my choices? They were evolved men, after all, both in relationships with strong and independent women. Surely they wouldn't hold it against me if I told them that I too deserved a chance to make my own life a success?

Armaan was away, again. He had taken Ekta to the Maldives to celebrate her birthday. When he had told my parents he was going, they looked at one another disapprovingly, finding it easier to cast that expression between themselves than on their grown-up son who was in a sophisticated, modern relationship. In our circles, all men took their girlfriends off on sexy, exotic holidays, whether they were married or not –something that would never have happened a short generation ago.

I went into my room and, from my closet, pulled out the large poster board I had stashed in there when all this had started. Back then, I had scrawled the names of the potential male heirs, their strengths and weaknesses and what, as far as I knew, they were individually working on. Cold fusion. Military drones. Liquid natural gas.

Months ago, I had known nothing about any of this. Now I knew a little. Not enough, but something. Still, I had to find my own thing –

not piggyback on what one of my male relatives was doing. I stashed my poster board back in my closet and opened up my laptop. I referred back to my email exchanges with people I had met in Los Angeles on a trip I had taken on Milan's behalf. My cousin, as far as I knew, hadn't pursued anything I had presented him with. By the time I had come back, and had started to fill Milan in on the possibilities I had investigated on his behalf, he had begun his dalliance with the beguiling actress, Anushka, his ambition sidetracked by her tempting invitations to join her on shoots in Lausanne and Rome.

I looked at my notes. There had been a conversation with a Delhi tycoon who was a recent Beverly Hills transplant and who was seeking funding for a movie. High risk, high return, he had said. Baba would never take it seriously. Baba tended towards ideas that were real, grounded. He was a steel man at heart. He would want something he could touch, not something fanciful that dreams were built on.

I had gone to see Jag on that same trip, encouraged by Nitya who had thought it was about time I had 'closure', if there was such a thing really. Over drinks, the last time I saw him, he had handed me a package that contained information about a revolutionary solar cell that was in development. I looked at the paperwork now, remembered the enthusiasm with which Jag had described the project to me – a product that was small and compact, yet could harness enough clean energy to power a home in a township where electricity outages were a daily occurrence. Something like this, I had to concede, would help millions of the working poor who needed power to watch the evening news, to allow their children to study at night.

If I wanted to pursue it, I would need to talk to Jag again. We would be back in each other's lives, in whatever context, and the thought of that was appealing to me, rich with possibilities. We would be allies towards a common goal and he would respect me again and that respect might lead to something else. It was a notion that filled me with hope.

Then, my eye fell upon a name card I had scanned in. Martin Veitch, CEO, Applied Automotives. I had liked him, had been excited by his idea – hydrogen-powered cars. He needed research and development money. His previous funding had dried up. Other car makers wanted to buy him out and the big oil companies were trying to shut him down, not wanting to see his blueprint for petrol-free cars come to fruition. When I had met him, he had run out of options.

I had understood his zeal immediately, appreciating his refusal to be bought out by companies that had more financial power than he did. I realized that it didn't have the humanitarian heft of the solar cell, that it was for an entirely different demographic – the city folk who could afford a car instead of having to rely on a rusty bicycle or their own callused feet.

Both options gave me a lot to think about.

'What do you think I should do, Dada?' I was sitting across the table from my great-uncle, Baba's only brother, at a small vegetarian restaurant around the corner from his home. He had told me how much he had liked the idli-sambar here and I thought it would be a pleasant change from his small, stifling flat, where I usually went to see him.

'I am pleased you are taking the initiative, Beta,' he said. 'I am not sure I can advise you. It has been many years since I have been involved in business.'

I didn't know how much I could tell him, how much he would absorb. He didn't even own a computer. When Dada was my age, the idea of a car running on water and plastic cards supplying power homes would have been considered the product of someone's deranged mind.

He blew his nose into a large white handkerchief; he had eaten too many chilies. 'I will only advise you this. Don't focus only on profit. And don't think of impressing people. Choose a vocation that will please you, something you care to understand, something you are content to live your life doing, whether in this competition or not. With that, my dear girl, all success is possible.'

'Thank you, Dada,' I said, letting him pick up the bill; a small pleasure for an old man. 'I know you are shy to hear it, but I really do love you.'

He reached over and pinched my cheek.

# FOUR

Dadi, my beloved grandmother, was the woman I wanted to be when I finally grew up, if God granted me all of my wishes. She was one of those rare women who knew when to be tender and when to assert herself, who expressed a surfeit of wisdom in just a few words. She wore French chiffon and Chanel No. 5 and opened her handbag each time she met someone in need. I was her 'putoo', her baby, her special progeny because I was the only female grandchild she would ever have.

So when my mother told me that Dadi had invited me to lunch, specifically iterating that it was just to be the two of us, I was as excited as I was perplexed. In all my twenty-seven years, I had never been out alone with my grandmother. There had been one time when all the ladies of the house had gone to a navratri havan together and I had accompanied Dadi home because she had developed a migraine in the middle of the ritual. But other than that, I only ever saw her playing the role of the stoic and kindly grandma, surrounded by relatives, warm and welcoming but never showing favouritism.

'Lunch? Alone with Dadi? Why?' That was the question I posed to my mother, who was spending the morning in her bathroom with an orange towel around her neck and some hideous, malodorous mixture on her head. Coiled up, her hair resembled a large mound of cow dung.

'Did I do something wrong?' I asked her.

'Of course not' she replied. 'What will you ever do? I just told her you had some plans.'

'Did she think I was a fool?' I asked her.

'Dadi never takes any family member out to lunch alone, so consider yourself a lucky fool.'

Dadi had a morning appointment in Bandra, so asked me to meet her at Hakkasan. I made sure to get there in plenty of time; Dadi was not a woman you could keep waiting. There was a reservation in her name. I settled myself at the table in the pristine, Zen-infused space and asked only for water.

She arrived right on time, in a mint green Chikan saree, champagne pearls and marquis diamonds in her lobes. Rich lady luncheon attire. She was old-school enough to eschew nonsensical two-cheek European kisses. I had just met her, a few days ago; there was no need for her to treat me like a long-forgotten friend. Still, I stood up when she walked in and moved to the outskirts of the table. She squeezed my arm and told me to sit down again.

I elected to forego the hakkatinis I usually got here and we ordered Perriers with lemon. I sipped and the bubbles scratched my throat. She didn't look at the menu and instead told the waiter to bring the hot and sour soup, the clay pot chicken, dim sum and rice for two.

'Enough?' she asked me.

I nodded. I wasn't here to eat.

'Tell me how you are, Beti.' She rested her elbows on the table, gently nudging back her place setting to make room. 'How are you keeping busy these days?'

I wished I was five again, when I could say anything – anything stupid, anything pointless – and it would be okay because I was a child and nothing more was expected of me. Now, I wanted to tell her everything, to garrison the empty air between us. I wanted to engage her. I wanted to impress her. But nothing I could tell her would do that. I thought it remarkable that the comfort with which I had sat with Matunga Dada, the ease with which I had spoken to him, did not exist here.

'I'm home a lot, with Mummy,' I said truthfully. 'Otherwise, I see my friends. I help a few of Mummy's friends with their homes, some projects here and there. I keep busy.'

Her gaze drifted off me, landed somewhere else. Food arrived, small hot baskets packed with glutinous mouthfuls.

'Now that London is finished,' she said, as if that iconic British city had dissipated in the middle of the night, when it was really my self-styled grand plans that had done so, 'what do you have in mind for the future?' It was an odd question, one I'd never anticipated her asking me. She speared a dumpling with her chopstick, spinning it in a tiny brown puddle of sauce.

This was my chance. My grandmother was giving me an opportunity. She wanted me to tell her the truth. But I couldn't tell my grandmother. I didn't want her thinking, 'Who does this girl think she is?' So I said nothing.

She took a sip of jasmine tea from a small porcelain cup. 'I never told you,' she said.

'What?'

'How much of myself I see in you.'

'No,' I said.

'You know about my family?'

I knew a few things. That her father had been a prominent dignitary and knew just who to pay off to get things done, much like the man she ended up marrying. Things were easier then because there were fewer bureaucrats on one's payroll and travesties were easier to hide. And there was tragedy in her past. Dadi's mother had been a troubled woman who had never left the house, who had been medicated to such an extent that nothing was real, not even the touch of her daughter's hand. Anywhere else, she would have been in an institution. But in those days, not unlike modern times, mental illness besmirched a family's reputation. So she was kept hidden. She was a chronic sleepwalker; she would rouse at night and ambulate through their airy Juhu house. One morning, her body was found lying face down in the ocean, her stomach swollen, her long black hair billowing around her head. She was hauled in like a cache of rancid fish. Nobody ever spoke of it again. Dadi was only eleven when it had happened.

Now, looking at my grandmother's serene face, I pretended not to know anything. I feared that if I told her what I already knew, it would clog the connection between us, whatever there was of it.

'My father, he was a Rai Bahadur. A man of high standing. I was his eldest and a disappointment. A man like him was supposed to have had a son. But there was me, a girl. And then later, I only had boys. And my boys only had boys. Except for you. You came to us for a reason.'

I was glad I wasn't drinking. My grandma was confusing me enough. I felt like I was on a date with an especially cryptic man.

'Your grandfather is a good man,' she said.

The waiter arrived with the clay pot, releasing a blossom of steam into the air when he opened it.

'But he is not an easy man. He has had to fight many battles. Everyone thinks that things came easily to him. They did not. We Badshahs have had to struggle for everything. It is our naseeb.'

I closed my eyes, absorbed her words. She parsed her language, like grandmothers do, but I understood her perfectly.

'Badshah Industries started with a woman,' my grandmother said. 'And there's no reason why it should not continue with one.'

Despite what she was trying to say to me, it was as if my grandmother was hiding behind a wall of deference to the boys of the family. I felt like a young woman in love, seated opposite a man who has planned a perfect marriage proposal and then gets cold feet and keeps the ring in his pocket, those much anticipated four words, 'Will you marry me?' evanescing over the petits-fours, the flat champagne, the silent violin strings. Dadi wouldn't commit to me, at a time that I needed her to.

I wanted to say something of consequence, but no words came out; the words, questions, pleas for help, were locked in my head in a muddled chain. I wanted to talk to her about solar cells and water cars, about dreams and destinies and if it mattered that I was a woman in the male-driven dynamic of my family. I wanted to tell her of my insecurities, and ask her how I could break out of them. But it seemed too free, too bold, and, where my Dadi was concerned, I didn't think I was either of those things.

Instead, I looked at her, my gracious grandma in a beautiful saree, taking small sips of jasmine tea and telling me her story. I realized that I didn't know how to overlay my story onto hers.

On the way home, while Rohit was cursing under his breath about the traffic-jammed streets, Milan called. I had told him I would be seeing our grandmother for lunch and he wanted an update.

'I don't really have anything to report,' I said. 'She talked to me about her father. She asked me about my day-to-day life. That was it.'

'Well that sucks,' said Milan. 'I thought maybe she'd have some insight into what's going on with our crazy grandpa.'

'I'm sure she does,' I said quietly. 'But that's hardly something she would share with me.

'She did say something interesting though,' I continued. In the background, Milan stopped tapping at his keyboard. He claimed to be answering pressing emails, but I was quite convinced he was downloading porn.

'What?' he asked.

'She said that Badshah started with a woman and there was no reason it shouldn't continue with one. Any idea what she was talking about?'

Milan paused for a second. 'I wouldn't pay her any attention,' he said, the clacking of computer keys starting up again.

'I did want to talk to you about something else,' I said. I had been waiting to tell Milan about my decision to formulate some kind of plan for the business as well. I knew he'd ridicule me – as fond as Milan and I were of one another, there were still plenty of moments when he didn't take me seriously. I'd been waiting for a chance for us to talk in person, but he seemed to have so much going on these days, what with his other business endeavours and infatuation with Anushka. Perhaps this was as good a time as any.

'What's up?' he said

'Well, I've been meaning to ask you – the leads I brought back for you, from LA – were you planning on pursuing any of them?'

'Why?'

'Didn't your mother tell you it was rude to answer a question with another question?' I teased.

'Didn't yours?' he teased back.

'Are we going to get anywhere with this conversation, Milan?'

'I don't know,' he said. 'Are we?'

'Okay, I'll be the grown-up,' I said. 'Here's the thing. I've been thinking…' I heard a faint beep from my phone, telling me my battery was close to depleted. 'I thought maybe if you weren't using those ideas, I might…'

The line went dead. I resolved to call Milan back the second I got home.

# FIVE

As soon as I walked through the door, Chanoo told me that Jaanvi had called, inviting me to the opening of her friend's new home accessories store in Fort. Her mother-in-law was supposed to accompany her, but had cancelled at the last minute, claiming something more demanding had come up.

I wondered if it might have been Vivek Abbas' libido. I thought back to an evening in early April, after Vivek's triumph at a cricket match, when I had seen my aunt press her long red nails against his shirt. With his perfectly round bottom, tight abs and manly features, not to mention his ferocious style on the field, he had fascinated the nation's women. Magazines had anointed him Bachelor of the Month, Most Beautiful Man and the rest. But Malini somehow knew him. Malini was close to him. Her fingertips had been on his shirt.

Jaanvi, the wife of my only married cousin, now trusted me, considered me a friend, if not a sister. We had stumbled into a new and tentative relationship, a late start really, given that she had been married into my family for more than three years, that we weren't that far apart in age and that I was the closest thing to a sister-in-law she had within the clan. I felt ashamed that I had so readily dismissed her, that I had thought her restrained personality to be doorknob-dumb, her unremarkable appearance to be a reflection of apathy. I had only recently initiated a friendship with her and only because Milan had goaded me to find out what Jaanvi's husband, Sharan, had in mind to win the company. The whole thing had been mean-spirited and debasing.

Thankfully though, Jaanvi and I had struck up a genuine mutual fondness. She never suspected the real reason behind my overtures to her or, even if she did, had pretended she didn't.

I told Chanoo to call her back and tell her that I'd meet her at the party and rushed into my room to get dressed.

'These people will go to the opening of an envelope,' I said to Jaanvi, as we merged with the crowd inside the store. 6 p.m. on a weeknight, in a city notoriously hard to get around in, and the place was packed to the ochre-tinged walls. Not that these people had shown up to finger fine linens and sniff Indonesian patchouli candles. They were here because the younger sister of the designer who had just opened the store, Cadence Collections, was the lead star in the hot TV serial of the day, a perky-breasted girl who could devolve into on-screen histrionics at the wave of a peacock plume. She was the girl that everyone wanted to see. She now stood in a corner, posing for photographs in a silver, sequined mini dress, all Kareena Kapoor-esque pouting.

'She's got fat knees,' I said to Jaanvi, pointing out the offending limbs. Jaanvi smiled but only for a second. She pulled me to one side, next to a wall showcasing overpriced magenta dupioni cushions and Vietnamese lacquerware. She put her hand on mine and moved her head forward so close I could smell the peach pulp in her shampoo.

'I don't know who else to talk to, Soh,' she said. A tear slipped out of one eye.

'What's going on?' I asked her, genuinely concerned. Jaanvi was one of those rare girls in high society Bombay who never engendered jealousy among the ranks. She was rich, yes, and wealth could create all sorts of enemies, as I'd seen, but she wasn't a glamour puss, like all the other girls with whom we associated, which made her a non-threat, a fleshy nondescript chunk of abalone in a sea of well-manicured piranhas. That and the fact that she was warm and kind, precluded her from the tiny poison prickles thrown around – 'She's put on so much weight', 'Is it true her husband has a mistress in Taipei?', 'Didn't she wear the same dress to the last kitty party?' The girls of our ilk left her alone. Perhaps too alone.

'Things are bad between Sharan and me,' she said 'I want to leave him.'

A divorce? It had never happened in the history of the Badshahs. And if Baba had anything to do with it, it never would. Marriages around us were cracking like thin-shelled eggs, but we Badshahs pulled through, no matter what. I glanced around the store, at the happy smiles thick with fakery, the heavy wallets being fished out of Dior handbags, the credit cards being handed over for yet more frippery that would languish unused.

'Shall we leave?' I asked her. She nodded, pulling a crumpled tissue from under her sleeve.

We settled into the backseat of her car. Neither one of us felt like going anywhere. She needed to sit and talk and not be bothered by waiters or worried about the possibility of running into a friend. She gave her chauffeur money for dinner and sent him away. Inside the car, she didn't turn the lights on. I heard her crying. 'I don't know what's wrong with him,' she said. 'He barely talks to me. Some days, he won't even look at me.'

It wasn't that long ago that I was with Milan at Dome when we happened to see Sharan in deep conversation with his secretary, Mary. Milan, he with the virtually animalistic instincts, immediately locked into an affaire. 'Of course they're bloody boinking,' he'd said, with typical Milan bluntness.

Knowing Sharan as I did, I wouldn't be surprised. He was just a little too aloof, too superficial to know how to really connect with a woman, even his wife. It did not help that she was not his first choice, would not have been even his hundredth. Baba had selected her, to take Sharan away from the frolic of girls with whom he was cavorting. Jaanvi was from the requisite 'good family'. She was not an exhibitionist – far from it, in fact. She was prime daughter-in-law material. And it mattered not one bit to Baba that she wasn't the sort of girl that Sharan wanted.

I had told Jaanvi none of this – not my observations about their mismatched alliance, not even about seeing her husband with another woman. It wasn't my place. I didn't know enough.

'What are you going to do?' I asked her. It seemed the easiest, most harmless question. With it, I could avoid her having to ask me what I thought.

'I love him,' she said. 'But this whole thing with Baba, the fight for the company … it's made him crazy … he's obsessed. If he doesn't get it, if he loses, it will destroy him. It will destroy us. Maybe I should just leave before that happens.'

I lay my head back against the headrest. This was it, over and over again. Baba had no idea what he had started the day he'd told his grandchildren to wage war with one another for control of the company. He saw it as healthy competition. For these men, there was nothing healthy about it. But at least she'd said nothing about an affair. Couples can recover from quarrels over money, over power. But to have someone else involved, a heart lost to an intruder … there's no returning from that, not really, not ever fully.

'You can't leave.'

'Nobody would care,' she said. 'I could go back to Lagos, be with my parents.'

'Don't be pathetic,' I said. I surprised myself with how unsympathetic I sounded.

Jaanvi turned back to face me, switched on the overhead light. In the harsh, concentrated glow, she looked terrible. Her eyebrows were unkempt. She was wearing no make-up. The solitaire diamonds in her ears shone brightly.

'Seriously? Your husband is a bit aloof and you get ready to pack your suitcases? If every wife in Bombay behaved like that, the town would be overrun with divorced men.'

'So? What do I do?' she asked, tearfully. 'I hate this. I hate being ignored by him. I know he never loved me at the beginning. But I was hoping he had started to. Things were okay. We talked a lot. We had fun. And, in the bedroom ... it was good.' She blushed slightly. 'But now, there's nothing. We don't talk. We don't go anywhere together. At night, he doesn't touch me.'

'It's a phase,' I said, pointlessly. 'It's a phase and then it will pass. I don't think leaving is the answer. Not now. You have to stay and fight for him. Sharan will come to his senses.'

If there was one thing I knew about Sharan, it was that he did honour his family's reputation, which is why he had married Jaanvi to begin with. That Mary, she was nothing more than a busty plaything who made up for Jaanvi's obvious aesthetic shortcomings and she might have been willing to do a few more tricks between the sheets. But Sharan would be bored of her before long. He bored easily.

'He's your man,' I said. 'Do what you have to do to keep him.'

The words left a bitter taste in my mouth; they left me thinking of Jag.

# SIX

It had been a long time since I'd dreamed of Jag, the wavy-haired, highly evolved, deeply sensitive, uncommonly compassionate man who I was once convinced I'd marry. After we had broken up, I had to jettison him out of my thoughts; he didn't belong there anymore.

But on a foggy summer morning, I did think of him. The talk with Jaanvi the night before – of her estrangement from her husband, her feelings of isolation – got me thinking of just how good I had had it with Jag. Here was a man who'd showed me over and over how much he loved me, whose loyalty I had never doubted, until his father talked him out of marrying me because of something that had never had anything to do with me.

I got out of bed and drew the curtains. The air conditioner rumbled gently, wisps of condensation patterning over the window. The last time I had seen him, in San Francisco, he had kissed me in the lift. There was a note of finality to it. He had not asked me to stay, had not said he was sorry, had not wanted to take it all back. Whatever I had been secretly hoping for on that trip, did not transpire. In spite of being madly in love with him, I had no choice but to walk away, to seal up the crevices in my heart with a forced indifference.

Later, when I was back in Bombay, we had talked again. I had told him that Armaan was now in the running as well, having lost his thriving ad agency to his thieving, defrauding business partner. Jag had suggested that I turn Armaan onto liquefied natural gas, a potential investment in a plant in Azerbaijan. I had done so. But I never did ask Armaan what he had decided to do with that information. By then, there was Ekta, the girl my brother was convinced he would marry. These Badshah boys, I thought to myself, would forever be undone by gorgeous girls.

Still, that night at Privee, when I had made the decision to have a shot at the company as well, Jag had been the first person I'd called. I had felt no estrangement then. We clicked right back into place. His voice had been filled with warmth, he understood what I needed to say without my having to say it. As I talked to him that night, I knew it would have taken very little to fall in love with him again. I just had to hold myself in check.

Now, as the household came to life outside my bedroom door, I ran a bath. It was okay to not have a love interest right now, I told myself. It was almost edifying, to not want to lose weight for this man or that, obsess about which dress would cling to the bosom just so, to be mindful of when to flirt and touch and tease and when to be the girl that their mothers would like.

For as long as I could remember, there had been boys. Hot boys who were not to be trusted. Boring boys who would make fine husbands but to whom I would run out of things to say after the honeymoon. Married boys who should have married me but chose not to. Divorced boys who frightened me a little, but were desperately appealing anyway. Clueless boys, whose attempts at seduction involved a poke in the back and a drunken whisper, 'you wanna?'

And then there was Jag. Sure, he was handsome and of the rare kind who could be trusted. He was never boring; his mind probed mine in ways nobody else's did. I never felt more myself than when I was with him. Losing him devastated me.

I realized I should be trying to manipulate a time and place where we could meet, where he could fall for me all over again and think nothing of the directives of his stern, betrayed father who hated my family because they had cheated him on a business deal.

I had launched into this whole process of winning the family company, so I could right the wrongs that had been done to the man I loved. But perhaps, by then, the wrongs would be too far ingrained. He wouldn't love me anymore, no matter what I did, and our passionate few months together would be relegated to some grainy snapshot in his mind. I was going to be someone he could occasionally recall fondly and that was all. So whatever I was doing, however many relationships I was upsetting, I needed to do it for me. I would have to be content that he would be in a corner, cheering me on, wanting my success not for him, but for me.

I poured bath salts into the tub and swirled the water around with my hand. The day was just beginning.

Later, it was Karan's birthday – lunch at Wasabi. Like for all family gatherings, it was important to show up, to take time away from hair appointments and business meetings and personal trainers and charity committee meetings to attend the celebration of one of our own.

Today Malini was there, of course, front and center as Sharan and Karan's mother. She was wearing a hot pink dress with an abstract print scattered across its front. Her hair was big, Malini style. Her lips were lined thickly, as if to hem in the gloop of gloss that covered them. The waitress came around with cups of green tea, shots of sake and crisply fried tempura and served with a sprinkling of soy sauce. I looked around the table. Everyone was here. The family was united again. The family was happy.

I took a seat next to Jaanvi. Sharan was on the other side of her. Milan grabbed the seat next to mine, literally pushing out my younger brother, Rajan, who grumbled loudly about wanting to go home anyway.

'You never called me back,' Milan said.

'Oh. Right,' I said. That day, after lunch with Dadi, I had meant to tell Milan about my decision to lobby for the company as well. But what with the drama with Jaanvi, I simply hadn't had the opportunity.

'It sounded like you wanted to talk about something important,' he said.

'Sort of. Maybe chat later, after lunch?'

'Can't,' he replied. 'Leaving for Bangkok right after. Business.'

'When you're back, then,' I said. 'Nothing urgent.'

'Look,' Milan said, distracted again, drumming on the table with his chopsticks. 'Have you realized Karan has spent his entire bloody birthday lunch on his mobile?'

I turned to look at the birthday boy: he had excused himself from his seat and was by the entrance to the restaurant, his iPhone pressed hard against his right ear.

'He should seriously have that thing surgically attached to his brain,' Milan said. 'I'm sure his solitary brain cell would appreciate the company.'

We both laughed and had another swig of wine. I had to hand it to Baba. Despite viscerally fracturing the family like he had, setting cousin against cousin, brother against brother, we all knew well enough to still come out to play together. There were air-kisses, gifts in prettily-wrapped boxes with glittery bows, things that Karan neither needed nor wanted nor would ever use. Glasses were raised, a cake was cut, smiles beamed across the room and bounced off the walls. The boys would go home, burrow into their paperwork, tell one another lies, find secret ways to nab the empire. But looking at us now, we were one, big, happy family.

At least for today.

# SEVEN

The next morning, Armaan came into my room without knocking. I sat up in bed, rubbed my eyes, pulled my blankets over me. I was wearing a satin camisole, a remnant from my Jag days and felt awkward in my big brother's presence. He was holding the newspaper, waving it front of my face.

'Shit,' he said. I could smell Marlboro on his breath.

'What?'

He flung the paper down onto my bed. My eyes went straight to Manjuli Khosla's byline. It had been more than a week since I had talked to her. Something was bound to come out, sooner rather than later.

'She knows everything,' said Armaan. 'Baba's going to friggin' lose it.'

I picked up the paper to read the story quickly. Manjuli, to her credit, had gotten every detail right. She had laid out the facts as I had told them to her. I was cited simply as 'a source'. She had kept her word.

'It was going to become public eventually,' I said to Armaan, hoping to God I didn't look as guilty as I felt.

My brother picked up the paper to read the article out loud to me. 'In a shocking turn of events, Darshan Badshah, tycoon philanthropist and the founder of Badshah Industries, has informed his three sons, Amit, Jeetu and Prakash, that none of them will be entitled to inherit the family business, even after he steps down or passes away.

'Instead, he has told his five grandsons that they should each try and win the business. According to a source close to the family, Badshah senior has put to his grandsons a bold and daring challenge. They must each come up with a ploy that will take Badshah Industries to the next level. He will choose the best idea and best business plan and will then select the next CEO. The move is bound to send shockwaves through Mumbai's close circles of high net worth entrepreneurs, many of whom also run family businesses.'

Armaan looked up. 'How the hell…?' he asked me. 'Who is this source?'

My face felt sweaty.

'Dad's going to be so pissed,' he said, snatching the paper and leaving my room.

By the time I emerged from my bedroom, ready for breakfast, my father was gone. It was Sunday. He was always home on Sundays.

'He had some things to take care of,' my mother said, contriving to ignore my gaze at the breakfast table, her eyes overcast. My phone rang several times during the day; I didn't answer any calls. I only wanted to speak to Milan. He didn't respond and he didn't call me back.

The blowback from Manjuli's newspaper story was tremendous. Newspapers across the country piggybacked on to Manjuli's scoop. The article was reprinted everywhere. There were editorials about it, spin-off features about the long-term viability of any private family business. One weekly even ran a Badshah family tree, the headline reading, 'Who Will Win?' with boxes dedicated to each male cousin, outlining what they had to offer and painting my father and his brothers as base and doltish. After all, these editors reasoned, in a culture replete with sons who inherit, why were these men disavowed that right? My mother's friends called, claiming to be so sorry, it was all such a travesty, is Baba thinking clearly?

My mother and I went for a walk to Priyadarshini Park, our special refuge in the city. It had been a long time since we were here together. She grabbed my hand, like she used to when I was a child.

'We were hoping to keep all this private,' my mother said. 'Now, everybody knows. All your papa's friends. They know that he's not good enough.'

'But Chacha Amit and Prakash aren't good enough either,' I said. It was small consolation. It wasn't going to matter to my father that his own father thought all his sons were crap, not just him.

A child skidded by on a tricycle, his mother bunching up her saree and sprinting after him, a three-year old anxious to escape his over-protective mother who was afraid he would fall and hurt himself. She should be told that it would never end. That toddler will one day be thirty and his mother would still chase after him, wanting to keep him safe.

I was wearing chappals and the grass prickled my toes. Walking with my mother meant really walking, a slow, dilatory process that wasn't so much about getting from A to B as it was about the process, the measured steps, the quiet breaths, the private conversation, just my mother and her only daughter enclosed in their own little world.

I had violated my family's privacy because I had needed something from a journalist who, in the whole scheme of things, meant nothing to me. And the thing that had motivated me to make the deal with her – months earlier, she had given me some private information about Jag's father's feud with my uncle – was perversely antiquated now. I didn't even care about it anymore.

'First I thought,' my mother said, picking up the pace a bit, letting go of my hand. Her breath was laboured. 'First I thought that, in a way, maybe it's a good thing. So should Baba be shamed.'

'But then,' she continued. 'I saw your father's face. It's a terrible public humiliation.' She shook her head, fell into silence.

'Do you think it might rain?' I asked, staring skywards. When all else fails, change the subject. This was my perfect opportunity to tell my mother the truth. We were out in the calm of nature. There was nobody else around. Surely, I should tell her that Manjuli Khosla got the information from me?

But in so doing, I realized, I would necessitate a whole load of things. I would have to tell her about Jag, the great love of my life. But telling her about him now would also reveal that I had never told her about him before. And then, I would have to tell her how he left, and why. What Uncle Amit had done, at Baba's behest. I would cast even more of a shadow on the family she had always thought to be beyond reproach. I realized I just didn't have the guts, and had successfully convinced myself it was best to leave things alone.

'Well, the men, they have to get over it,' my mother said. A thin shroud of sweat covered her forehead. 'What's done is done. They have to make their way in this new world. Even if it means that a son will be a father's boss.'

She stopped walking for a minute. 'What you said, the other day, are you still thinking about it? That you too wanted to try to win the business.'

I nodded.

'How, Beta? With what?'

Legitimate questions. All the others had had 'proper' college educations in America; Sharan and Karan had both gone to Ivy League schools. All five of them, in their own ways, were brilliant: Sharan was shrewd, Karan was gutsy, Armaan was a hardwired entrepreneur, Milan was quick-witted, Pawan was an unmitigated brainiac.

And what was I? Relatively attractive. A good cook. Popular, cheerful, kind. I could redesign a room in my head in five minutes flat. But none of that was going to make me a CEO of a billion-dollar corporation. None should.

My mother, however, was astonishingly intuitive and always forthright. My father had told us that he knew she was the right woman for him when, on their first time out alone together, she noticed he had been overcharged at the restaurant, had asked to speak to the manager and got him his money back. This, despite her knowing of the wealth of the man she was going to marry. 'I knew then that if she could stand up for me when it meant so little, she would stand up for me when it meant everything,' he had told us dreamily, on more than one occasion.

So, in the dull morning spotlight of her gaze, I knew that my mother knew everything, on some level. And in that moment I felt like a fool, like a child, like a liar.

'I have to try, Mummy,' I said quietly. A knot gathered in the back of my throat. The tears would follow.

'I'm not sure how, but I will have a plan,' I said. 'Even Dadi, when we had lunch, said that Badshah Industries started with a woman, and with a woman it should continue. Don't you think she meant me?'

My mother raised her hand to my hair, smoothed it down gently and smiled.

'I don't know what she meant,' my mother said. 'Your grandparents are mysterious, both of them. I cannot tell you what to do. If you feel this is your way, then go, do it, try. I will be here.'

We started for home.

# EIGHT

First thing the next morning, I texted Jag. We hadn't talked since the night of my epiphany. He had told me to let things settle in my head, to give myself a little time, figure out what I wanted to do and then to call him again. His last words to me – 'You can do this. I will help you.'

He suggested we chat on Skype. He was working from home. I needed more time before I was ready to speak with him. It was Skype. It was visual. Unless I figured out how to disable the camera in my laptop, I needed to get out of my pajamas, do my hair, put on some make-up. Even though he had seen me at my worst, retching over a toilet bowl, that had occurred when we had become a 'we' and I could just be me. Now, it felt like we were strangers again. I tried to tell myself I no longer had feelings for him. But I couldn't let him see me in my morning disarray.

Twenty minutes later, his face was on my screen, a shadow of stubble over his broad, smiling face. His black leather chair squeaked as he moved. He picked up a coffee mug inscribed with his initials, a small red heart at their center. I wondered who had given it to him.

'Good to see you,' he said, his eyes crinkling kindly. 'How are you?'

I fidgeted with a pencil, mumbling something about being great and that all was well. I was distracted by how good he looked. From some musty alcove in my memory, I recalled the scent of his body. He was thousands of miles away, yet he was in my bedroom and I suddenly yearned for him. Skype was a miracle. Skype was a curse.

'Where you off to so early?' he asked.

'Huh?'

'You're wearing lipstick.'

'Oh, right. I have an appointment. After we talk,' I lied. He couldn't know I'd put on make-up to speak to him. He would never countenance the artifice of it.

'So, where are you with things?' he asked, all business.

I craned my neck, looking behind him, hoping to catch a glimpse of the shadowy space in the background.

'What are you doing?' he asked.

'Oh, just being nosy,' I said. 'I wanted to see what your flat looked like.'

'In the first place, we call them apartments here,' he said. 'Nobody in America knows what a flat is. And seeing as you're so curious, shall I give you the grand tour?'

'Yes, please!' I said, clapping my hands.

'Are you sure you have time?' Jag asked drily, unplugging his laptop so he could walk around with it. 'I mean, I don't want to make you late for your appointment. The one you put on lipstick for.' He beamed sexily into the screen. I knew that he knew that, below my bias-striped Michael Kors top, I was wearing pajama bottoms.

He walked with his laptop through the flat, flipping on light switches, showing me a well-kept living room – beige couches, printed cushions, neat floor rugs. There was a small dining space containing a round table, that seated four, beneath a low, funky brass lamp, a wine rack in the corner and a Bose stereo system. Adjacent to it was an open kitchen, where I would imagine that Jag, the wondrous cook that he was, spent a lot of time. From hooks hung a series of copper pots and there were tall fluted bottles of oils and vinegars, a glass container crammed with wooden spoons and slotted spoons and silicone spatulas in a rainbow of colours.

'My humble abode,' he said. 'That's pretty much it.'

'Where's your bedroom?' I asked.

'Oh, we're going there, are we?' he said, just a little flirtatiously.

He walked down a short, white-walled corridor and into a room. He turned on a slender floor lamp that cast a beam of light upwards, radiating onto the crisp, compact space: a bay window, the twinkling lights of the city beyond, dove grey bedding, a series of black-and-white prints on the wall. For a second, I indulged in imagining myself there, occupying this home with him, opening the oven to check on the dinner, rummaging through a drawer for the corkscrew, fluffing the pillows on our bed, pulling the curtains apart in the morning, paying bills at the dining table. Keeping house. Like a young couple in love.

And then I saw it. A toiletry bag, on a chair beside the bed, made of pink batik, a canister of hairspray sticking out of it. Next to it, a floral printed silky nightgown. Women's stuff.

My blood froze. I didn't want to see it, I wasn't prepared for it and it shocked me. It shouldn't have. Jag was an attractive man and women would want to be with him. But I didn't want it thrown in my face, that he had moved on – and maybe a girl had moved in – when a part of me was still holding on to some tendril of hope that one day, he might be mine again.

He seemed strangely nonchalant, like it hadn't even registered what I had noticed, like surely there was nothing to explain, as though that part of our relationship was done with.

'Okay, let's get on with it,' he said, moving back into the living room and settling down on the couch. 'Tell me what you're thinking.'

I had to reset my head, remember what I had called him for. I reached for a bottle of water, took a quick glug and tried to compose myself. I thought, first, that I might disconnect, telling him I'd get back to him. But I had to power through. We were where we were. In the few minutes it had taken him to walk me through his flat, we had crossed over from lovers to friends, unequivocally, irrevocably. Someone else was occupying the spot in his life once meant for me. I could shed some tears later. Now, I had to pull myself together. We had business to take care of.

'I was looking at the solar cell project you told me about,' I said, holding my voice firm. 'When I saw you. At the Mandarin.'

'Oh right,' he said, recognition flickering on his face. I wondered if he remembered that last kiss. It probably didn't matter anymore.

'I think it could be fantastic. A great business idea and could do a lot of good.'

'It could,' said Jag. 'Problem is, the last I heard, development was halted. Funding was cut off. I think the patent for it is still in existence though. Depends on how keen you are to get it all going again. I can probably find the right contacts for you.'

'Oh,' I said, mildly disappointed; I was facing a wall. Did I want to try and scale it? I looked at Jag's face, his good intentions reflected in his eyes. My pursuing the solar cells idea would mean continued communication with him. It would mean my relying on him, perhaps even collaborating with him. It would mean that the sudden need to detach myself – a need brought on by a chance view of girlish accoutrements in his otherwise masculine bedroom – would be more drawn out than need be.

'It's okay,' I said. 'Sounds like too much trouble. Maybe I should consider the second option.'

'Which is?' he asked.

'The hydro-powered car. The Vecco. I met the guy in LA I told you about it.'

'I remember. I looked at the company. It seemed viable.'

'I liked the guy behind it. He seemed like he knew what he was doing. Not that I've even gone back to him. Things might have changed. Also, when my grandpa made this announcement, it's not like he gave us a set of rules exactly. He said to bring him something. But what? Just an idea? A business plan? Or an actual business, signed, sealed, delivered?'

'I can't answer that question,' said Jag, sensibly. 'But of course, the more work you do, the better. The more it looks like a sure thing, the higher your chances.'

He rubbed his chin thoughtfully. He looked tired, like he wanted to watch TV and eat honey-roasted peanuts in bed. I remembered how good that felt, with him.

'So what do I do next?' I asked. 'There's a prototype. The company needs funds to start production. Do I ask my dad for money, try and buy him out?'

Jag leaned back in his chair, chuckled a little. 'It's not that easy, Soh.' He rattled off stats off the top of his head – Warren Buffet spent more than US$200 million for a minority share in a Chinese maker of hybrid cars. And then there was the patchy history of Tesla, despite all that money poured into it. These were nascent technologies, he said. And they required big, big money.

'Look, I know enough about your family to know that if they wanted to take over the guys behind the Vecco, they could. With one cheque,' he said. 'But you're not your family. Not for this purpose, anyway.'

I scratched my cheek. A smear of foundation came off under my fingernail. I had never before put on foundation before taking a shower.

'What, then?'

He closed his eyes for a second, like he always did when he was thinking. 'I have some thoughts,' he said. 'I'll email you in five. Stand by.'

The line disconnected abruptly; I stared at the screen now bereft of his face. In a flash, he was gone. I was left wondering if I would hear from him again, left feeling almost like I did the day he walked out on me in London. Like this time he was gone. Really gone.

When his email finally arrived, two hours later, it was long and involved. Tired as he looked, he had spent all that time working, helping me. I hated him for being so kind. I wanted him to be a jerk so I could get over him easier.

He had sent me links to newspaper stories about acquisitions in companies that made eco-friendly cars. Then, another link to a business website in the States, that had interviewed Martin Veitch about how he had almost signed with an investor in Chennai, and how that deal had fallen through at the last minute.

Underneath that, Jag had written, 'These guys want to be in India. If you can give them access, you can score yourself a deal.'

I read the material he sent me, three times over.

The next night, Jag called me. A straight phone call, his landline to mine. It was his morning. I wondered if the woman was there.

'An old college buddy of mine is on a consulting gig in Mumbai. He's super-smart. A shark actually. I'm gonna text him, ask him to help you with this.'

'Oh, that's sweet, Jag,' I said. 'Thank you.'

'No big deal,' he said. 'He moved there with his girlfriend. Maybe you can show her around.'

'Of course,' I said. 'I can't thank you enough.'

# NINE

Mary Verghese sat in the fourth pew on the right side of St Michael's Church, clutching the marigold garland she had bought from a street vendor outside, its golden petals crushing into her white skirt. It was late and the church would soon be closing. She had decided to linger for a while after the day's final recitation of the Novena, grateful for the silence that had begun to descend upon her, relieved that the throngs of people who packed this place every Wednesday had finally left, back to the wretched lives they had come here to transform.

Mary had scuttled out of the way for those in wheelchairs, had stared at the curdled skin of the leucoderma victims, had shuddered at the emaciated frames of the cancer-inflicted. She had sat in this brine of despair, willing herself not to absorb the sadness in the hall. Later, when it was time to walk home, she would breathe in deeply the night air, exhaling all the impurities she may have inadvertently allowed to settle in her cells.

Mary might have been born Catholic, but she was not a religious person. Far from it, in fact. Sure, she wore a tiny gold cross around her slender neck and would accompany her righteous, God-fearing parents to Christmas mass, but she had never really embraced the whole Jesus thing. How could she, if she was going to be involved in an adulterous relationship and be on birth control – sins not just in the eyes of the Lord but something that would no doubt cause her mother to condemn her to an eternity in hell. Mary, after all, was Indian, middle-class, lived at home with her parents, was born a Catholic; there was nothing in there that would have predisposed her, or so it would seem, to participate in a steamy relationship with a wealthy, famous married man.

But Mary saw herself as none of those things and didn't care to be middle-class for much longer. In Mary's world view, much more could be accomplished through means other than prayer. Prayer, she had decided, was for the weak, for the hopeless, for those who believed some non-existent entity was the only conduit by which their dreams could come true. But desperation has a way of converting even the most hardened atheist.

Mary had dreams too, and so far, her strategies for turning them into reality had failed. She was in love with a man who was married to someone else, albeit unhappily, but still, there was no divorce in the offing. She had tried everything to make Sharan want her enough to leave that plain, uninteresting woman he was stuck with. She had tossed out her birth control pills, believing quite resolutely that she could conceive the child Sharan so ardently wanted and, in doing so, would guarantee herself a place in his future. She came from fertile stock, after all; she had four siblings, her parents were each one of nine. She could get pregnant in no time, if she wanted, unlike that useless Jaanvi, who was as barren as the Mongolian steppes of the Gobi.

But Mary couldn't just wait for the triumph of conception. She had to stay proactive. She had initiated an ambitious number of the positions illustrated in the compendium of the Kama Sutra that she had surreptitiously ordered. She had taken a class in massage therapy so she could relieve Sharan of his many stresses. She threatened him with ultimatums, then soothed him with sweetness. She had tried to back off, like all those articles in the women's magazines advised, to play hard-to-get, to not be so available. So far, nothing had succeeded in making Sharan want her enough to leave his wife.

Still, Mary knew she had more than a fighting chance. She spent more time with Sharan than anyone else, knew the most minute details of his life. There were moments when they were sequestered in their own private world, in the curtained, quiet cool of a five-star hotel room, when they would lay together on the fine white sheets and Sharan, tipsy on champagne, would whisper to Mary how much he loved her. As the moon glowed outside, he would place his hand on her belly, and, with his arm draped lazily behind her head, he would tell her that he could imagine the two of them entwined like this forever. He just had a few things to take care of. He was under so much pressure now, trying to take what was rightfully his. He had a lot on his plate, what with all the turbulence in the business, his foolish cousins, his thick-headed brother. Each time Mary heard this, the injustice of it all angered her. She was going to do everything she could to make sure Sharan won the company and, when that happened, she would be right next to him, sharing his splendour.

This was why she was here now, on a hot and humid Wednesday, the air inside the church still sweaty from the people who had swarmed around her, discomfiting her contrived serenity.

Mary's friend, Xavier, was her Konkani-speaking Catholic conscience. He was from a stridently religious Goan family who had lived next door to the Vergheses for years. Xavier loved Mary as he would a sister, would love her more if she would ever let him. Xavier's mother, the portly Mrs Fernandez, had begun to display signs of early dementia. She would forget where she left the tea cosy or would pick up the phone to call someone and have no recollection of who it was that she had wanted to speak to, and, just the previous week, had got on the train at Byculla and couldn't remember where she was going. There had been the mood swings, the dark bouts of depression. Mr Fernandez, Xavier's patient and quiet father, knew what he was up against; when his mother-in-law had died, her mind had been a mess. He had known then that he was going to lose his wife the same way.

But then Xavier heard about the Novenas at St Michael's Church, a ritual that drew thousands every Wednesday. The common belief was that a church-goer would visit the institution for nine

Wednesdays in a row to recite the Novenas and by the end of that time, their most profound wish would be granted. Xavier had heard too many tales not to be convinced – the office-worker who beat his colleagues to a promotion, the reclusive bachelor who prayed for an accommodating wife who wouldn't expect too much of him, the newlyweds desperate for a small flat of their own. Blindness vanished. Bloated tumours deflated. Failing hearts were made whole again. Xavier, like so many people who flocked to the church, needed to believe that a miracle could happen for him, too.

It was on week five, on his way to church, that Xavier came to call on Mary and had invited her along. She had initially balked at his suggestion; she had had a long day at work and wanted to relax in her tiny room at home, hoping that perhaps Sharan would call for a last-minute rendezvous.

Xavier joyously told Mary that the disintegration of his mother's brain had slowed. She had cooked a foogath perfectly, just as she had done as a young bride. She had put down her glasses at night, and had known exactly where they were in the morning. She was no longer so depressed. Surely, he told Mary, if such wonderful progress could be charted after just five weeks, imagine what another four would bring?

Xavier wanted Mary to come because he knew she had been struggling in a relationship. He was not aware of the details; he would never have held Mary in such high esteem if she had told him that the subject of her affection was a married man. As far as he was concerned, there was a man she admired from a distance, yet obstacles stood in the way of their togetherness. Xavier had assured Mary that her commitment to the Novenas would result in the Lord coming to Mary's aid. If Mary wanted her happily-ever-after, this was the way to get it.

It was the end of the evening now, and the thirteenth and final recitation of the Novenas had taken place an hour ago. Xavier had left, needing to run to the market to fetch fish and coconuts for his mother.

Mary had said the words, which now still seemed to echo in the room. She sat heavily in the pew, afraid to move, fearful of dislodging the eerie peace that the chanting had brought. The words themselves were meaningless to her – 'come holy ghost creator blest and in our hearts take up thy rest come with thy grace and heavenly aid to fill the hearts which thou hast made' – and she was aware she had recited them with a cold detachment.

But she was here. Perhaps the difference would be evident as early as tomorrow. Perhaps she would go to work and Sharan would greet her with open arms, kiss her longingly on the lips, in front of everyone. He would tell her he was leaving Jaanvi, that he and Mary were fated to be together.

Maybe Mary wouldn't need to return here for the next eight weeks; maybe the Holy Mother, after whom she was named, would grant her wish much sooner than that.

# TEN

*I am sitting on an old rocking chair, looking out over the lawns in front of my home. Beneath my feet, the tiles are cool. A black, spotted dog from the house next door has come into our garden, and sniffs the plants I have made grow. He lifts his leg and urinates on the herbs I planted with my own hands. I smile. That is okay. I am by now used to seeing the things that are mine being pissed on.*

*The other day, I took my granddaughter out to lunch. I had never done that before. In all my years as a well-known lady of Bombay society, I have taken many people out to lunch. Too many. For example, all the ladies – the ones I had grown up with – with whom I had celebrated wedding anniversaries and the arrival of grandchildren and sat next to at markas when their husbands died. I have taken strangers out to lunch – the founder of a new charity or some big shot at Jaslok or a woman whose minister-husband had suddenly become important to my own husband. In Bombay, there is never a shortage of reasons to host a lunch.*

*But I had never taken out to lunch one of my own daughters-in-law, not even my only granddaughter.*

*Later that afternoon, I met my friends for a game of rummy. One asked me where I had just come from. Hakkasan, I replied.*

*'Oh?' asked my nosy friend Bhagwanti. 'With who?'*

*'Sohana,' I said.*

*'Acha?' She raised a thin grey eyebrow. 'Why?'*

*I suppose that they would have delighted in hearing that I thought my granddaughter, as fond as I am of her, to be a very silly girl. Sohana annoyed me at lunch with her childishness. I was there with her, alone. She could have told me anything, asked me anything. But she seemed more interested in the ingredients of the clay pot chicken than hearing from me.*

*When her mother had called me and told me what Sohana had said, that she too had her eye on the business, I felt thrilled. 'Finally', I thought to myself. The girl is showing something more of herself. She has good instincts. She knows right from wrong. She is a family-minded girl. She will do anything for us. I have tried to tell her before,'do not think less of yourself because you are a girl.' She too is a Badshah. Now it seems the girl has woken up. She has seen something in herself.*

*But there we were, eating dumplings, and she said nothing. It was as if she expected me to hand over everything, like an expensive dish on the Hakkasan menu. I was going to do no such thing.*

*In my mind, a girl needs to be smart enough to know who to go to for help and humble enough to ask for it. That will be the first lesson my granddaughter will learn.*

# ELEVEN

Bharat Malkani had a goatee, a slender gap between his two front teeth and a voice that made me think of aged cognac and fine silk dressing gowns. When he called me to introduce himself, I was a little taken aback. When Jag had said 'an old college buddy', I had assumed his friend was an American, a white guy named Tyler or Ben who would be elated at the opportunity to spend a year in exotic, exuberant, booming Bombay. I did not anticipate a fellow Indian whose mother, as it turned out, was somehow related to my aunt Preeti's brother.

This was the small kernel of information that fell out onto the table as we launched into a second round of Colombian Breeze cocktails – a fruity, yet heady, sangria served at Escobar, a place assumed largely to be named after the infamous drug lord.

'I'm up for anything that suggests narcoterrorism,' Bharat had drawled, on the phone, when I had suggested it as a meeting place.

So now we sat, picking at tapas, circling around one another. The small talk had been dispensed within halfway into our first round. By the time his drink was drained, the chit-chat was officially over.

'Where's your girlfriend?' I asked him.

'Around.'

'Oh. Sorry. Sore subject?'

'She turned psycho when we moved here.'

'Sure,' I said. 'It's always the girl's fault.'

Her name was Tania. They had dated for almost two years. They had met at Bharat's previous job, in Singapore, where he was in venture capital. She worked in legal affairs at the same company, two floors below. Their relationship blossomed over late night cappuccinos and corporate picnics. She had started talking about marriage. He wasn't interested. She was pushy. He retreated. He wanted to end the relationship. She always found a way to keep him hanging on.

She got transferred to Bombay. That should have been his exit; a miraculous reprieve.

'She talked me into coming with her. She can be pretty persuasive.' He twirled a cocktail stick between his fingers. Tania found him a job, through a friend of a friend, India-style nepotism. Her new job came with a flat. His did not.

'I gotta tell you, man, living with her opened my eyes. She got, like, seduced.'

'By what?' I asked.

Bossa Nova played in the background. Around us, flames quivered inside chunky pillar candles.

'This town,' he said. 'It's crazy. She was a pretty sensible girl before we got here. I mean, she likes clothes and stuff. Parties. Which girl doesn't? But here, she went nuts. Like she had to be a part of every goddamn thing.'

Tania was enthralled by her new friends, the scene, the bars, restaurants, endless parties where dinner was served at 1 a.m. She kept telling him how much fun it was, how much he was missing out by wanting to stay home and read John Grisham. He moved out, into a one-bedroomed service apartment in Worli.

'I think calling her psycho is a bit extreme,' I said. Tania's life sounded a lot like my own, once upon a time. 'She sounds like she's outgoing, is just having a good time. She's in a new city. What's the big deal?'

'You don't know the whole story,' he said, snapping the cocktail stick in half. 'If you did, believe me, you'd be calling her psycho too.' He downed his drink. 'So,' he said, suddenly sitting upright. He was done talking about her. 'Jag tells me you need a little help with a business thing. What's the deal?'

I told him. He stared sideways at me. Guys like him require very little information, just the basics. They fill in the rest. Jag was right. A couple of drinks in a bar, some chit-chat about a supposedly sociopathic ex-girlfriend and I could see how smart the man was.

'Okay,' he said. He yanked out the cocktail napkin from under his drink, dabbed at the moist ring at its center, pulled a pen from his pocket and started scribbling.

'The company I worked for in Singapore, it was a branch of a huge, multi-armed Washington firm. We did this kind of stuff all the time.'

'It's okay,' I said. 'You don't have to sell me on who you are. Jag says you're good.'

He stopped scribbling, looked up at me. 'So what's the deal with you and him?' he asked.

'Why do you ask?'

'Just curious. I get that you guys are friends. But he has a ton of friends. He doesn't go out of his way to help that many of them.'

'We dated. In London. Last year. But he had to go back to San Francisco, and I had to come back here.' The less said, the better.

'He always had a way with women, that guy. If he was into a chick it was guaranteed she'd be into him too. He just has that thing. You know?'

I knew.

'Anyway, back to this,' he said. More drinks arrived. He started scribbling again.

Later, I offered to drop him home. While we waited for Rohit, he pulled out a packet of Winstons and waved it at me. I shook my head. He lit up, inhaling deeply. I stared at him, wanting to get a good look under the street lamp, as he preoccupied himself with his puffing. His hair was cropped short with spikes of silver peppering his sideburns. From the side, his nose was Romanesque. He took another drag. There was something in him that reminded me of Milan, the sort of man who didn't care what others thought of him, needed nobody's validation. I found that vaguely thrilling.

Rohit arrived. Bharat stamped out his cigarette. In the car, he recited his address, with directions, in flawless Hindi. He had grown up shuffling between the US and Singapore. His fluency in Hindi took me by surprise.

'Bet you didn't know I could do that,' he said.

'I didn't,' I replied.

The aroma of tobacco and musk wafting off his body hit me now, even though I'd spent two hours next to him in a crowded bar. Here, there was no sensory overload, just he and I cruising down a Bombay street, late at night, alone. A daub of tapenade sat at the corner of his lip. I reached out to wipe it away. He touched my wrist. I caught Rohit's eye in the rearview mirror and pulled my hand away.

We slid up outside his apartment building.

'Nightcap?' he asked quietly.

I wanted to say yes. I didn't want to go home. I wanted to be alone with him.

Rohit raised his eyes to the mirror again, catching my gaze.

'Better not,' I said. 'It's late.'

'Okay,' he said. 'I hope you got what you needed.' He opened the car door, sliding one lean leg out.

'For now,' I said, letting him place a cool kiss on my cheek.

# TWELVE

I woke up thinking of him.

If Rohit had not been around, judging my every move, I would have accepted Bharat's invitation to go upstairs. I'm not sure how far I would have let things go but something would have happened, that much I knew. How could it not? His emotional inaccessibility was alluring to me, as was his coolness, his bravado. Bharat was all shades of grey and quicksilver. He didn't fit into any convenient categories. He wasn't the typical bad boy, but certainly not the good boy either. Not knowing who precisely he was made him exciting to me. That was more than I could say about anybody I'd met since Jag.

I threw off the covers and got out of bed. From my purse, I pulled out the paper napkin. I looked at it now, smudged with black squiggles. So this was how Bharat Malkani conducted his affairs.

My phone rang. It was him. My heart skipped. I lay back down in bed.

'Hey,' he said, his voice raspy. 'Just wanted to make sure you got home okay.'

'You're about ten hours late,' I teased. 'I could be lying in a ditch somewhere. You know, if you want to check on a girl, you call the night of. Not the next morning.'

'Point taken.'

'I was just sitting here, looking at whatever you scrawled on this scrap of paper. Seriously? People pay you for this stuff?'

'A lot,' he said. 'The napkin usually costs extra. I threw that in for you.'

'What do you want, anyway? You didn't really call to check up on me.'

'Free for lunch?' he asked. 'I'll order in.'

This time, I took a taxi.

I had never been inside a serviced apartment before. This one had a pair of teal blue couches positioned severely across from one another, as if being readied for a state visit. Copies of *The Economist* and *Newsweek* were strewn across a basic coffee table. An air-conditioner rumbled loudly overhead. It felt cold and stale and lonely.

'Sorry it's not up to your exacting standards,' Bharat said, as my eyes took in every detail.

'It's not that,' I said. 'It just feels a bit ... well ... sad.' The inside of a crematorium, I imagined, would feel more cheerful. 'Do you really like it here?' I asked him, sitting down.

'Sure,' he shrugged. 'I didn't have to think of cushion covers or bedspreads or where to put a chair. I just unpacked.'

'Yes, but it's like nobody lives here.' There were no framed photographs, no special mementos from a trip to Cambodia or Mykonos, nothing to distinguish this flat from the one next door, apart from the smell of tobacco that was embedded in the walls.

'I'm not here much. Just a place to sleep in, at night. Anyway, I hope you like Italian,' he said, disappearing into the kitchen. He emerged with two plates, heaped with salad, pasta with sausages, crostinis that dipped soggily in the middle. He set the plates down on the dining table and returned to the kitchen. I heard the gentle pop of a bottle of wine being uncorked, glasses being filled. We sat down.

'Cheers,' he said, clinking my Chardonnay against his. 'To cars that run on water.' He took a sip. 'Do you have any questions?'

'What are you? My college professor?'

'You went, did you?' he asked. 'You don't seem the sort.'

I coiled some spaghetti around my fork. It reeked of garlic.

'Jag gave me some background,' he said. 'About you. Your family. Before we met last night, I googled you.'

'Well that's reassuring,' I said. 'What conclusion did you reach? That I was some soulless, blockheaded heiress?'

'Is that how you see yourself?' he asked.

'I think that's how people see me.'

'Not everyone. Jag doesn't see you that way. I might. But what do you care what I think?'

I leaned back in my chair. 'Why am I here?' I asked.

'You tell me,' he said.

'You invited me,' I said. 'Why?'

'We weren't done talking last night. You seemed in a rush to leave. You wanted to come up here, but you didn't. You were more concerned with your driver's opinions of you than what you wanted. That's a bit pathetic, isn't it?'

I hated him. He was smug and self-involved. He was no Jag, my sublime ex with his syrupy sweetness, amenable persona and heart flushed with goodness. Bharat was one of those guys that Nitya would not hesitate to call a 'jackass'. There was something of him that reminded me of so many of the Bombay boys I knew – untouchable and unassailable, protected by daddy's money and mummy's social connections. After having been exposed to Jag's authenticity, his uncommon kindness, Bharat was like a cold slap in the face.

But I was here, at his dining table, alone in his flat. And still, he made me want to do things I had not wanted to do since Jag.

Now, I suddenly had an overwhelming need to get out of here. I saw how this would end. I knew men like him, had trained myself to avoid them. They were hardwired to cause women pain.

'I need to go,' I said, folding my napkin, my plate still packed with food.

'Where?'

'Home. I don't know. Away from you.' The wine had hit me. I needed to go.

He lowered his voice. He put his hand on mine; it was surprisingly calming.

'I'm sorry,' he said. 'I can be a jerk sometimes.'

'You think?' I said, sarcastically.

'Please,' he said, stroking the back of my hand with his finger. A stream of shivers cascaded down my spine. 'Don't go.'

I didn't.

# THIRTEEN

Two days later, I called Martin Veitch, at 11 a.m. on a Wednesday morning, Los Angeles time.

'He's vacationing in Solana Beach this week,' the receptionist said cheerily. 'Is it urgent?'

I glanced at his card again. His mobile number was on it. I always resisted dialing the mobile number first. I figured if I needed to talk to someone, I'd rather they be at their place of business, ready to work, not driving or ordering pizza, or toting kids around. Out-of-the-blue calls on mobile phones were, to me, an unwelcome intrusion on everyday life.

'I'll call back,' I said. 'But here's my number, just in case.'

I hung up and looked at the cocktail napkin again. I couldn't be bothered to transfer Bharat's notes into a more conventional format, like a Word document. I left them, as they were, on a slightly crumpled and partially moistened six-by-six inch square of double-ply paper.

I thought about the afternoon at his house and my stomach lurched. His fingers were long, had felt waxy when he glided them across my shoulder. His goatee had chafed against my cheek. When he kissed me, it was hard, as if he couldn't believe I would yield to him. But I did. The scent of him called to mind whisky and pain. He had started to unbutton my top. I had grabbed his hand in mine, held it down. For a second, he had flinched, like he couldn't believe the audacity of it. Then, I had felt his muscles relax, his hand give in to the pressure of mine. He stopped. I had given him enough.

Now, my phone rang. I snapped back to where I was. It was Martin Veitch. Some vacation.

'Do you remember me?' I asked, realizing how stupidly unprofessional the question sounded as soon as it was out of my mouth, as if he was some guy I'd met on shaadi.com.

'Sure!' he exclaimed, all Californian openness and warmth. 'We talked when you were in LA. What's up?'

'What's up?' didn't seem like the most propitious way to kick off business negotiations.

'Have you found what you need?' I asked him. I was sure he had. Companies like his had tangible things to offer, things that would save money and build communities and enhance life in general. Smart people would be investing in those ideas. Surely, by now, people had invested in his.

'We're in talks with a few folks,' he said. 'Nothing signed yet.'

'Maybe I can help,' I said.

'What's your plan?' he asked.

'Hang on,' I said. I swiveled the cocktail napkin around so I was staring squarely at it. I cleared my throat, forcing an officiousness into my tone that was not ordinarily there.

'I want to buy rights for India. Plus a volume-based royalty.' Bharat had underscored those words on the napkin. 'The idea is to manufacture here, yes?' I asked.

'Of course,' he said. 'Based on previous negotiations with a potential Indian partner, we did our due diligence. We could have production up and running in no time. There's a factory we can work with. In Gujurat.' He let his tongue roll over the word: goo-joo-rat.

'Okay,' I said.

'I can email you a proposal in the next couple of days,' he said.

'Fine. I'm sorry about bothering you on your vacation.'

He chuckled.

'No such thing as a real vacation anymore.'

# FOURTEEN

The invitation was the size of an iPad and probably cost as much. It was a silver card with the heft of a suit of armour, embellished with brilliant sky blue lettering, tucked into a lush, silk envelope.

It was for the sangeet party leading to the wedding of the year. The town regurgitated every shard of gossip that emerged around it. The twice-divorced Dipo Chadha was about to take a chance on marriage number three, this time with the large-breasted, auburn-haired Kalpana Tharani. The questions on everybody's lips alternated between who had more money and how long the union would last. If bookies were in action during Bombay society wedding season, this was the one to bet on.

With good reason, too. Dipo Chadha loved alcohol. He drank it. Distilled it. Sold it. In unwholesome amounts. Rumour had it that he supplied a number of Arab fiefdoms with illicit alcohol. He procured women for them, too.

Obscenely wealthy sheikhs who tired of the maidens they regularly recruited from obscure Eastern European townships and who were often in the mood for a little dark-haired exotica, had Dipo on their speed dial. He had girls galore he could dispatch over on the next Emirates flight, girls happy to be wined and dined, to be danced and played with. To do whatever needed to be done. Everyone in Bombay knew what Dipo Chadha did for a living and it didn't matter. What mattered was that he was stinking rich. And the money, unlike that of so many other Bombay boys, was all his. At least whatever was left of it after he paid off two excessively disgruntled ex-wives.

Kalpani Tharani, however, was another story. She was like the young, buxom Mother Teresa of our community. She didn't have a malicious cell in her body. She was the queen of virtue. With that cleavage and that complexion, she should have been married at twenty-one. But she was too busy, her mother repeatedly and vociferously complained, 'doing good'. Like that was a bad thing.

'Hai Ram, my Kalu, again she's gone to feed the poor,' her mother would say to my mother, when they would meet at some society shindig or another. 'I keep telling her, "Beti, if you are only with poor people, how will you meet anyone normal?"'

Not that the Tharanis needed their daughter to marry well. Kalpana's father, Nirav Tharani was one of those 'industrialists', like my own grandfather – a word that seemed to encompass anything that had to do with building empires and, occasionally, destroying lives. There was a college named after him. He owned supermarkets in Indonesia and oil refineries in Africa and a lot of things in between. He and Baba had lunch every few months, with a few other heavily-monied men, no doubt discussing how they would eventually take over the world.

So Kalpana couldn't have been marrying Dipo for his money. She certainly wasn't marrying him for his kind heart – he didn't have one of those. Personality? Rolling out dry chapattis was more fun than talking to this chap. So what, then?

'It's better than being single,' Nitya observed. She was at my house, refreshing her make-up as we dolled up to go to the party. 'Speaking of which, I hope there are some decent guys there tonight. Aren't you tired of just hanging out with girls all the time?'

I thought of Bharat, at what happened at his house the other afternoon, at my snowballing feelings for him and I felt a little thrill. I would tell Nitya about it later.

Within the hour, we arrived at the Chadha home in Walkeshwar. It was the sort of place you'd see in an elaborate Karan Johar movie, all stately columns and diyas bobbing on placid pools in the courtyard. I almost expected Shah Rukh Khan to come bounding down the front steps in some tennis ensemble, all dimpled cheekiness, kissing his mamma as he zoomed off in a black Porsche to woo Katrina Kaif. It was a spectacle of the grandest proportions; waiters in red-and-gold turbans, fireworks streaking through the sky, tables heaving under the weight of kababs, korma and eighteen different types of chaat, big-biceped men in tight suits, sunglasses and earpieces – both families had hired bodyguards, the big new trend for the much-monied – striding around.

'If bride and groom are wearing matching outfits, I'm going to slap them,' said Nitya, lifting up her lehenga as we walked into the palatial living room.

'Go ahead. I'll Instagram it,' I said, indicating Kalpana and Dipo, who were reclining on fat golden pillows, the pair of them in midnight purple frippery, looking like charred eggplants under the hot, bright lights.

'Crap, look at that bloody necklace,' said Nitya, grabbing my hand, clearly forgetting about the wardrobe transgression. A piece of jewellery would have to be especially astounding for Nitya to comment on it, so accustomed was she to seeing dagger-sized emerald earrings and solitaires the size of an infant's head.

Indeed, it was hard not to notice Kalpana's necklace. It stretched from just under her chin to where her copious bosom began, an endless rivulet of diamonds, alternately studded with cabochon rubies. It was as grotesque as it was compelling, the sort of ornamentation worn by a Masaai tribeswoman, with D Flawless gems instead of wooden beads.

Kalpana spotted us and waved us over. She stood up to greet us; I was surprised she could keep her head straight with that bejeweled monstrosity weighing her down.

'Looking gorgeous,' Nitya said to her. 'Like, wow.'

'I'm so happy for you,' I said, taking Kalpana's hand. I tried hard to mean it. She and I were the same age. She had bolted down her fears – the fears that must have risen when agreeing to marry a man like Dipo Chadha – and seemed determined to make it work. It was bold and admirable. I could only envy her. Even if the marriage devolved into some abysmal disaster – and how could it not? – at least she could say she tried. I had never even been proposed to.

'Thanks,' she said. Speckles of gold shone brightly on her pretty face. She looked hopeful and that made my heart swell.

Dipo stood up too, probably the thousandth time he had to do so that evening.

'Ladies,' he said, all bearded charm and faux bonhomie. He was dashing. I had to give him that. He was as eligible as eligible bachelors could be, all that height (six-foot-two) and British accented geniality. Despite his muddied personal history and his immoral business dealings, Kalpana's parents were taken by the fact that he spoke flawless Sindhi, had recited Urdu poetry to their daughter on their second date and had, of course, that monstrous bank balance. Fake charisma and gargantuan wealth could assuage many misgivings.

'Please, grab a drink, get something to eat,' said Kalpana, gently nudging Nitya and me towards the bar, the typical gambit of hostesses who need to be getting on with something else. 'We'll party later, okay?'

That was when I saw him.

# FIFTEEN

'I figured you'd be here,' Bharat said, slinking up to me, holding two tumblers of Scotch. He handed one to me. I wasn't a whisky drinker, but I took it anyway.

'Why's that?' I asked.

'Superficial people. A pointless display of obscene wealth. Kind of seems like your thing.'

'Piss off,' I said.

We hadn't talked since that afternoon, at his apartment, when I had let myself give in to him, just a little. I remembered the vigour and confidence of his kiss, the certainty with which he slid his palm behind the nape of my neck and drew me to him. I had left before we went any further.

This had happened four days ago, and there had been no communication since then.

I hated how irritated I felt, how I had begun thinking of him all the time, checking my phone obsessively to see if he had called. Try as I might to be a modern girl, to have flings without much thought, I wasn't. I ached to be like that, someone who could be with a boy for a night and forget about him by morning. It was all the rage in Bombay these days, to be a vixen, to lob for cheap thrills. I got unduly attached to men, even those who I knew, on some level, would end up hurting me. Nitya had said it would be my downfall, that I needed to play it cool, develop thicker skin.

'Chill,' Bharat said now, his dark eyes piercing mine. 'Have a drink.'

We both turned to look towards the crowd. This was my fifth wedding event over the past month. Our lives, typically, were filled with them – small, sweet ones at the local temple, the bride and groom described as 'bechare' by my parents because they couldn't afford to fly in entertainment from Miami. And then these mammoth affairs, all ten-carat diamonds and wedding planners and outlandish themes. As if a theme would help a marriage last. As if a theme would make a groom a more faithful man, a bride a more tender wife.

A screech from a microphone caught everyone's attention; something was happening.

'Ladies and gentlemen,' said the emcee, a shiny-suited fellow who, with his dyed-black bouffant, looked like a young Rajesh Khanna. He was alone atop a gleaming wooden stage, constructed on the long green lawns of the Chadha home. 'On this momentous occasion, the sangeet celebration of our Kalpana and Dipo, we are thrilled to introduce to you…' He stepped back. Silence fell on the crowd. In a town where gossip spread like melted margarine, nobody knew who the entertainment was tonight.

'…Black Money!' he burst out joyously, into the microphone.

The rapper appeared from behind a silvery curtain. I recognized the slippery red leather outfit he was wearing; he'd worn it to the Grammys, where he'd picked up three awards. Black Money – could a name have been more appropriate for the event, the people who populated it and the city in which it was being held? – was the hottest rap star, in the league of Jay Z and Kanye and 50 Cent.

Eardrum-bursting music exploded over the speakers, Black Money belting out his latest hit, 'Do Me Right, All Night,' the kind of thing that would play in a strip club, not here, at a swanky Sindhi sangeet, for a supposedly virginal bride. Dipo stood up, yanked Kalpana off her gilded bolster, led her to the dance floor. Others followed, awkwardly gyrating to the music, trying to find a rhythm in its cold throb. Kalpana's father, a small man with a fleshy face, pulled his wife up, plunged his hand into his pocket, yanking out a wad of notes to circulate them over Black Money's bobbing body, as if this Brooklyn-born black man would ever understand the significance of the ritualistic blessing of his art, the laying of money at his restless feet. The younger guests were too busy being drunk to know if they were having a good time or not, the older ones looked to be pining for another time, a time when they could sway languidly to the soulful tunes of Jagjit and Chitra, or Ghulam Ali, who sang of the anguish of love, who told stories that our people could understand. But now, these same old couples, they danced and danced, trying hard to be cool. This, here, now, with all the Cristal and Johnnie Walker Blue Label and platters bloated with Junglee Meat cooked by chefs flown in from Rajasthan, I doubt if anybody felt anything meaningful at all.

'Want to go somewhere a little quieter?' Bharat said, motioning to a stone fountain at the far end of the grounds. A few people stood around it, smoking.

We walked in silence across the dewy lawn, the soft, wet ground yielding beneath my shoes. We sat on the rim of the fountain. I turned to look up at the sculpture at its centre, a pair of dovetailed fish, currents of water pouring forth from their upturned mouths.

Bharat lit up.

'So,' he said, blowing out a thin wisp of smoke. 'How's it all going with the guy in L.A?'

What did I expect? That he would ask me how I felt after our make-out session on his couch the other day? Was Bharat Malkani the kind of guy who ever asked anybody how they felt about anything?

'Okay, I guess. He's sending me some stuff to look over.'

Loud chatter, cheers and applause from across the lawn. Against all odds, Black Money was bringing down the house. Pretty indiscriminating, this crowd.

'At some point, I need to ask my parents for the money,' I said.

'That part is easy,' he said.

I didn't want to talk business and was disappointed that he had dragged me across the grounds for it. I wanted to talk to him about other things: him, me, what had happened the other day. What he felt, if anything. Where I stood. What I meant.

'Remember Tania?' he said. Of course. How could I forget?

'She's a lawyer. When you're ready, she can look things over..'

'Oh,' I said. 'So ... you're like ... back with her?' My skin prickled, my mouth tasted sour. I hated that I cared.

'God no,' he said. 'Are you crazy? I told you. She's psycho. But we talk sometimes. She can help with this. She knows her stuff.'

'Cool,' I said. 'Okay, I'd better get back to my friend,' I saw Nitya, surrounded by a cluster of shiny, gorgeous girls.

'Wait a sec,' he said. His hand was on my arm. 'I still want to talk to you,' His voice was lower now, softer.

'So, talk.'

'I'm sorry. I should have called you. After the other day.'

'You should have,' I said. 'Is that what you do? Act like a jerk and then apologize, figuring all will be forgiven?'

He flung his cigarette onto the wet grass, stamped it out.

'Being with you felt good,' he said. 'You felt good.'

My body turned warm again, but for all the wrong reasons. I wanted to leave here with him, right now. I wanted to be alone with him. The man was unattainable. He was a friend of the man I once loved, and they couldn't have been more different. Jag swept me up and I fit right into him, like a Russian nesting doll. Bharat was all angles and mystery, an infuriatingly complex puzzle. Men like him were toxic. He would cause me pain.

'I've got to go,' I said. My old friend, self-preservation, there she was again. This time, I didn't give in when his fingers tightened around my arm. I shook them loose and I ran off, like some distressed damsel in a B-grade Bollywood flick, the embroidered hem of my lehenga rustling across the grass.

I ran into Sharan, who was holding a plate of food – sea bass swimming in curried tomato, slender asparagus tips flecked with Parmesan, plumps of potatoes smeared with spinach. On his fingers he had a harness of rings – dense, glossy gold constellated with coral, symbolic for the pursuit of goals, emerald, for mental capacity, and sapphire, which supposedly facilitates the ushering forth of human destiny. With all that finger armour, Sharan looked like a pimp. The jewellery was new. The conclusion I drew – he had consulted with Gurdas, the family astrologer, roundly denounced as a buffoon by all, but someone whom Sharan had no doubt paid lakhs upon lakhs in order to pave his way in our depraved family battle. Gurdas was a proud believer in the potency of gem stones and prescribed them as routinely as a doctor would aspirin. Milan was convinced that Gurdas had deals with the top jewellers in town and got a cut when some waylaid tycoon sought a particular carat weight of a particular jewel.

Now, Sharan kissed me coldly on the cheek. Jaanvi stood at his side, wearing something pewter grey, perversely low-key for this rampantly profligate party.

'What's up, Soh?' he said, his American accent from his Harvard MBA days appearing at will.

'Oh, this and that.'

I was done. I wanted to go home.

# SIXTEEN

My mother, who had spoken to Preeti Chachi, was told that Milan had flown to Istanbul from Bangkok. More business. I needed to talk to him, but right now I still had to wait.

The next morning, Martin's business proposal arrived by email. On the face of it, what was expected of me was not hugely complicated. Money, primarily, but just an initial amount, to allow me to buy India-wide distribution rights to the Vecco. He told me to take my time, think about it, get back to him with any questions.

I knew that the first thing I had to do – the most important thing – was to secure the money I needed from my father.

I will concede that there are not that many girls in the world who can go to their fathers on a random morning and ask them for twelve million dollars. Even in my circles, where millions are routinely lost in an evening at the gaming tables in Las Vegas or Macau, any sensible parent would think twice when writing that kind of a cheque to an offspring – especially one who had yet to prove any sort of true ability.

Still, the request slid easily off my tongue, as if I were asking them for a second serving of rice at the lunch table.

'Say that again,' my father said, laying the *Times of India* on his lap.

A splatter of rain spider-webbed across the glass windows.

'For my bid. For Badshah. About that amount should do it.' A dewdrop of juice from the mango I was eating dribbled onto my chin. I realized I was being impossibly cavalier, that even to my own ears I sounded like I was joking. Perhaps there was a small part of me that didn't want my father to take me seriously. Jag had often told me I possessed a remarkable tendency to sabotage myself.

I had a plan and I would confide in my parents. Either they were going to trust me or they weren't.

'There's something I want to do that could be great for the family. For a lot of people, actually.'

I laid out the course of events – Milan dispatching me to Los Angeles, my own research, how I found Martin Veitch, my negotiations with him and what he was offering, what I wanted to buy ... I talked for nine-and-a-half minutes without stopping.

Armaan walked in, rubbing his eyes sleepily. My mother moved to vacate a spot on the couch for him. 'What's happening?' he asked, picking up the serious mood of the room.

'Your sister wants twelve million dollars,' my mother said. 'For a business.'

'That's a shitload of money,' Armaan said. 'Soh, what are you talking about?'

'Something to do with a car that needs no petrol, just pani,' my father said, looking as if he was trying not to laugh.

'That's actually a thing, Dad,' said Armaan, scratching the side of his head. 'What Baba said, about all of you boys having a shot at the business,' I said. 'I've decided I'm going to try, too. I heard about this water-powered car. I thought he might be impressed.'

Armaan said nothing, just stared at me, as if I'd told him I was signing up for sex-change surgery.

'If I give you that money,' my father said, 'what about Armaan? What if he needs money too, for whatever he's planning?'

'Are you down to your last twelve mil, Dad?' I asked. 'Helping me out – is that going to bankrupt you? Armaan, do you think dad has to choose between you and me?'

'I'm not saying that, Beta,' said my father. 'But money cannot just be thrown around like this. It *is* a lot of cash. For anybody.'

'Firstly, you're not anybody,' I said. 'And I wouldn't ask you if I didn't think it would be worth it.' My previously disdainful attitude dissipated. It was hard for me to ask them, it was hard for me to risk them saying no. Of course twelve million was a lot – it was a fortune. Most people in the world can work a dozen lifetimes and never see it. But it wasn't just the money I was asking for. It was an invocation for my parents to see me as more than their fashion-happy, party-hopping, perpetually single, eternally useless daughter.

'Dad, what Baba's doing, seriously, it's awful,' I said. 'Chucking you and chachas out like that. It's not okay. I can do something about it. I can increase our chances of keeping Badshah in the family, between us.' I was Wonder Woman without the pointy boobs, Batwoman without the peaked ears and flowing cape. I was going to right the wrongs that my grandfather was perpetuating against my father. In the end, that's what this was all about. I was going to be the saviour, a female, tan-skinned, slightly curvy Robin Hood. I was going to take from the rich and give back to the rich.

I was going to win the company back for my father.

'I have a proposal in hand, Dad. I just needed to make sure I could get the money. You can look through everything, if you want.'

My father took off his glasses, rubbed them against his robe. 'You know, Beta, you are the first,' he said, thoughtfully. 'Ever since Baba did what he did, issued that challenge, whatever you want to call it, I've not heard from the others. I don't know what they are doing. But at least you have a plan. Armaan,' he said, turning towards my brother, 'are you doing anything? Your girl, Ekta, is taking up all your time.'

'That's not true dad,' Armaan said, trying unsuccessfully to hide the defensiveness in his voice. 'I am looking at some projects. Just because I don't discuss everything with you doesn't mean I am sitting around on my ass.'

My mother, who had remained quiet through this exchange, as one parent often does when the other is so densely conferring with a child, finally spoke.

'Jeetu, give Sohana what she asks for,' my mother said. 'Consider it her dowry, if you must.'

'I wasn't planning on giving away twelve million American dollars as her dowry,' my father taunted, referring to me as if I wasn't even there. 'Whoever wants her should just take her.'

I rolled my eyes. I hated the conversation drifting towards this ephemeral wedding. And my mother, much as I loved her, much as I know she supported my every endeavour in her own way, should not have been equating my father's investment in me with my future marriage; one had nothing to do with the other.

'This is the most you've ever asked of me,' my father said, quietly. The alarm on his phone beeped; he had to be somewhere. He folded the newspaper, put it down on the table, looking mildly irritated that our conversation had prevented him from reading it cover to cover, like he usually did.

'I will do it,' he said. It rained hard. A wet flurry fell from the sky pattering against the pane. It wasn't cold, yet I wrapped my gown around me tighter.

'And I will do you the courtesy of not asking you anything further. I'm not going to ask you to show me anything. You tell me this is good, that it will bring Badshah Industries back to us and I believe you. You are my daughter; I trust you.'

I turned to look outside the wet, rain-battered window and continued drinking my tea.

Everything went into overdrive.

I called Bharat – putting aside my complicated feelings for him – and told him the funds had been secured. Martin suggested I go to Gujarat, to Sanand, near Ahmedabad, to look at the proposed factory and I took Nitya with me. Some of Martin's money had already been invested in the factory, from the previous deal that hadn't gone through, to begin small-scale production. We talked to Dev, the manager there, ignoring his bemused stare as my friend and I clattered our way up the metal spiral stairs in our high heels and fitted pantsuits, the pair of us black-haired Ivanka Trump clones. My brain fogged over when Dev told me about the dizzying number of permits that had to be obtained, forms to be filed with dusty, slow-moving government departments, but he wobbled his head genially, saying, 'no problem, no problem, I will take care of everything, you please don't worry, Ma'am', and I left there feeling reassured. But this was eventually going to be my turf and when I walked in here next, after permits were obtained and production started, the staff here would see me as the leader that I was.

Emails flew back and forth between Martin, Dev and me. I began interviewing for a sales manager who would connect with auto distributors around the country informing them about the Vecco. We talked time frames and quantities and pricing structures.

I felt an integral part of something important. I was caught up in a fevered rush, twelve million dollars worth of adrenalin – the best investment my father had ever made, I was sure, because he had made it in me.

By this time next year, business magazines would be charting my success as the new CEO of Badshah Industries. There was no way Baba would not choose me over my cousins; I was going to be the first to put forward an idea. I knew, based on what I had gathered of what the others in my family were doing, that all other projects were still in their infancy. Mine was real. People would be traversing the roads of my country in cars fueled by water, saving their hard-earned money at the petrol pump. Martin and I had already talked about taking the Vecco to other countries – Singapore, Malaysia, Sri Lanka. If I had learned one thing as a Badshah, it was to think big. When I had started all this, part of my rationale was to win back Jag's adoration. Now, that seemed trivial. I was in the midst of something so much bigger. Bharat had been an intriguing diversion, yes, but he was there as a sounding board, answering basic questions, resurrecting my confidence when it faltered.

I was going to restore peace to the Badshah household, to guarantee a spot in the company for my father for as long as he wanted it. I was going to be the daughter my father needed me to be.

Within days, a FedEx package arrived from Los Angeles, the familiar white, red and purple packaging screaming urgency – an overnight delivery. When Chanoo brought it to my bedroom, she looked at me with a slightly probing expression on her face, as if thinking, 'what could there possibly be for this girl to see that is so important?'

I shut the door behind her and punctured the envelope with a pen, reaching in and yanking out the paperwork. I stared at the blur of words, lines and lines and pages of them, words that on their own might have meant something but, strung together, were a load of nonsense. It was another language, and I had a complete incapacity to absorb it.

I had heard that Milan was finally back. When I called him, I was told that he was off getting a pedicure. I knew exactly where he was.

'You didn't call me when you got back,' I said, taking him by surprise as I flopped down on the empty chair next to him. 'There's stuff I've been wanting to talk to you about, need your help with.'

He had three women servicing him. As in life, so in the beauty salon, they fussed around him like he was an eighteenth-century Mughal princeling.

'I've missed you,' I said. 'How are you?' I sounded like a jilted ex-girlfriend.

He glared at me. 'I saw the goddamn newspaper story,' he said. 'I know it was you.'

One of the women trimmed a cuticle too close to the skin. He winced.

'Milan, listen...'

For a moment, I'd forgotten about Manjuli's piece. So much had happened since then. I'd met Bharat, had moved ahead with my plans for the

Vecco, had set my mind on becoming the winner who would take all. Manjuli's scoop had become just another piece of old news.

'That?' I said. 'Look, Milan, I can explain.'

He sat up. The white-coated woman at his feet, her hair in an oily braid, glanced upwards. 'I remember you talking about that Manjuli chick. You went to meet her. What did you think, that I wouldn't figure it out?'

'I had no choice,' I pleaded. 'She was threatening to publish a story anyway. It could have been much worse.'

'My dad can't even go to the Willingdon anymore,' he sneered. 'Says he's embarrassed to run into his cronies. And my mother, even with her goddamn psychology degree, can't do anything for him.'

'I had my reasons, Milan. Please, you know I would never intentionally hurt the family. It happened. We've all moved on. Why are you still holding this against me?'

'Well, I was about to forgive you,' he said. 'And then your brother texted me, told me about your plans.' He winced as the manicurist cut too close to the cuticle again. 'That you're moving ahead with the water car, the one you first told me about. Damn cheeky of you!'

I steadied myself. Armaan had no business discussing my plans with anyone else. 'Come on Milan,' I said. 'You didn't seem interested in the Vecco. So I figured it was fair game. And I've been wanting to talk to you. But you haven't been available. What was I supposed to do?'

My cousin leaned back in his seat. His handsome face, that carefully-cultivated stubble, the long eyelashes, the piano-keys teeth ... suddenly it all turned grey, angry. 'Seriously, Soh? You're blaming this shit on me?'

There were tears in my eyes now. Milan had never been mad at me before. Not even as kids, not even when we played. He always let me win. I didn't recognize this person.

'Look, you told me yourself,' I said. 'In your office. When you asked me to spy on the others. You said I was smart, that I knew stuff. Were you just lying then?'

The three women who were attending to him looked at one another, mumbled something about having to change the water in the bowls and bring fresh, steamed towels. They went off.

'No,' he said. 'I wasn't lying. There are things you are good at. You can make bhindi masala and chicken a la kiev. But this business stuff? Competing with us? Stealing my idea? Are you high?'

I picked up my bag and left, the contract from Martin still sitting inside, unseen.

I called Bharat from the car to angrily relay what had happened with Milan.

'Relax,' he said, his voice steady. 'Stop freaking out. Your cousin will come around. In the meantime, Tania knows all about this stuff. I'll call her. She'll help you.'

# SEVENTEEN

I knew she'd be gorgeous.

There was something in that name – Tania – that augured a high degree of foxiness. In any case, Bharat did not strike me as the kind of man who would ever date an average-looking girl. He didn't possess that sort of depth.

'So good to meet you,' she trilled, hugging me as if I were her long lost sister. Her hair smelled of vanilla and was so soft and fluffy that strands of it went up my nose.

We were back at Bharat's flat. Cups of tea had been laid out, along with a platter of aloo tikkis, as if some overbearing Sindhi mother had appeared out of nowhere. He'd ordered in, yet again, this time from the rotund Mrs Sahni, in a neighboring building, who had fashioned a neat business for herself, making heavy snacks and heavier main dishes for useless bachelor boys. She had brewed the chai herself, sending it over in a tall black thermos.

Tania occupied the couch opposite me. She sat board-straight, as if interviewing for a job. I knew that stance. It was generally exhibited by people who knew of me or my family and who were keen to impress. I remembered what Bharat had told me about her; socially ambitious, I think were his words. I knew where I stood in society and this girl could have done worse than to buddy up with me. It was clear she knew that.

Bharat and I sat on the same couch, but he had shifted to the farthest end, as if it were the only place for him, as far away as possible from his ex-girlfriend and sufficiently removed from me. Tania's eyes sprinted between him and me, as if appraising our acquaintanceship. I noticed, in the afternoon sunlight that slanted in through the windows, her face was flawless.

'What are these papers you'd like me to look over?' she asked, her gaze falling on both Bharat and me.

I lifted my bag off the floor, onto the couch and reached inside.

'Nice,' said Tania. 'Bottega Veneta right?'

'Yes,' I responded. 'Cruise collection. I saw it in Milan. Flipped for it. Love the weaving.'

'This is fascinating, ladies,' Bharat drawled. 'But can we just get on with it?'

'Ooh, somebody forgot to take their Metamucil this morning,' Tania replied, cheekily. I giggled. She and I shared a knowing glance over the coffee table. I could really like this girl.

I handed over the sheaf of papers. Tania took them from me, her fingers lightly touching my own as she did so. She glanced at the paperwork casually, as if perusing a Shobha De novel at Landmark.

'I'm going to take this home and have a proper look at it,' she said. 'Can I get back to you in a day or two?'

'Of course,' I said. I already liked her and I was grateful for her, for someone outside the family who had no vested interest in my success or failure. She had no reason to help me, not really, given that I was a stranger to her.

'I just want you to know how much I appreciate it,' I said. 'I didn't know who else I could go to. You know, while keeping everything confidential.'

'Of course,' she said, flicking her wavy bangs off her face. 'Any friend of Bharat's, is a friend of mine.'

I looked over at him, this passive participant, whose right leg seemed agitated. 'Thanks so much, Tania,' he said.

An artless sullenness fell upon us. It was as if Tania was waiting for me to leave, while I was waiting for her to do the same.

She stood up. As force of habit, and good manners, had taught me, so did I. 'It was great to meet you,' she said, hugging me. 'Get home safe.'

I picked up my bag. Clearly, I was the one who was supposed to leave.

Bharat stood up, too. 'Thanks again Tania,' he said. 'Sohana and I have some things to chat about. I'll ring you later, yeah?' He walked towards the door, bidding her to follow.

'Oh, right, sure,' she purred, picking up her bag, stuffing the paperwork inside it, following her ex-lover out. She turned to look at me as she went. That geyser of amiability that had greeted me had suddenly clogged, spluttered. The space between us turned arctic. She shut the door behind her.

Bharat sat back down in Tania's recently vacated seat opposite me.

'She was lovely,' I said.

'Stop.' He pulled a cigarette and lit up, his go-to when things got uncomfortable. His go-to, I thought, for anything at all. 'She's anything but lovely.'

'Come on,' I said. 'You were serious about her once. You must have seen something in her.'

'Sure,' he said. 'She's got a way about her. Guys love her.'

'You should tell her to run seminars,' I said. 'She's probably got some tricks the rest of us girls could learn.'

'Trust me,' he said. 'You don't want to know anything she could teach.'

'I can see why you drove her crazy.'

'Yeah? Why?' he asked, stuffing a tikki into his mouth.

'Because…' I said. 'Because there's something in you that pushes people away. People who want to be with you.'

'You're my shrink, now, are you?' He sat back in his seat, tapped his long fingers on his restless knee.

'No. But maybe you should see one,' I said. 'Find someone who specializes in intimacy issues.'

He stood up to walk around the coffee table. I shrank into my seat. I divined that Bharat was the sort of guy who may have a slight problem with anger management.

Without warning, he grasped my hand and plucked me off the couch, as if I were some reluctant weed that wouldn't yield from its earth. I wobbled upwards, stunned at the suddenness of his movements. He glided his arm behind my waist, pressing it against my back. I could feel the weight of it, of his body responding to my proximity. His mouth was on mine, not for the first time, but even more satisfyingly than before, deliberate, manly. He kissed me like Jag had. He kissed me like he really, really wanted to.

'Intimate enough for you?' he asked. I pitched backwards, dizzied by his abrupt fancy for me.

'Yes,' I mumbled.

'Just because I don't say things, doesn't mean I don't feel them,' he said.

'Okay,' I mumbled.

❖

It was one of those quiet mornings in the Badshah residence; Rajan was at school, Armaan had cloistered himself in the small office he had rented on Nariman Point, my father was at work, at a job he was unlikely to keep, and my mother was at the ladies' committee of some charity that had something to do with children. Or old people. I forget which.

I realized I hadn't checked my Facebook page in a while. Ten days had passed, but the lives of most of my 1,786 friends had remained unchanged. My friend, Payal, in Chile, exhorted her online buddies to 'PAAARRRRTY!' every

Saturday night, as if putting on a push-up bra and high heels and getting your hair blow-dried were just about the most fulfilling things in the world. Come Sunday morning, there were sure to be pictures of her plastered on Facebook, almost never with her husband, in some sultry one-shouldered dress, champagne glass in hand, her toned biceps and sculpted calves in full view. I used to 'Like' the photographs and make some inane comment about how fabulous she looked, but the compliments had worn thin now, so I desisted.

My annoyingly chaste friend, Lina, had posted some platitudes about life and spirituality and being a goddess of sorts, which was a little ridiculous because, before Lina had turned Buddhist, she had tempted her best friend's husband with just a little bit of adultery.

My mom-friends uploaded photos of their kids dressed as Superman for a party, bagging first place in some math contest, winning this race and that, wanting to be told just how cute their babies were, how adorable, how blessed.

I had friends who felt compelled to announce to one and all that they had just checked in at some airline lounge, to post pictures of themselves reclining in First Class, as if to say,

'I'm here. I've made it'. Milan and I used to laugh together at these posts; my cousin was often tempted to type out, 'Who gives a shit?' or 'You look fat', but I would smack his hand off the keyboard.

My phone rang. It was Tania. 'I looked over everything,' she said, her voice crisp and professional. 'It's pretty standard. Boiler plate, actually.'

'So, I can sign it?' I asked. 'And send the money?'

'There are a couple of minor amendments which I'll send over,' she said. 'But, yes, otherwise, it's a good deal. You can feel comfortable with it.'

'I'm really so very grateful, Tania,' I said, my voice weeping esteem. 'You have been kind to do this for me. Perhaps I can take you for lunch?'

'Sure,' she said. 'We'll set a date.'

The next morning, I instructed Raghu to wire twelve million dollars to the bank account Martin had specified.

Once Martin received the money, I told him I wanted him to be there at the presentation to my grandfather.

'Are you sure?' he asked. 'Sounds like kind of a private family thing.'

'I'm sure,' I said. 'I'll fly you in.' I was on a high. 'I feel so confident that even if Baba doesn't see the merits of it, if he goes another way, I still want us to do business together. I think it's important you're here, no matter what happens.'

'I'm honoured,' Martin said.

Then I had to figure out the rest of the guest list. This was still a private family event, not a big society party, but I wanted close friends there. Nitya, of course. And Anushka. Bharat, for sure. And I would extend the invitation to Tania, who had been so helpful. I went to see Matunga Dada, told him what I was doing and he smiled broadly as he held my face in his hands and kissed me on the forehead.

'Of course I will come, Beta,' he said. 'But the most important person for you is Darshan. Let him see the clarity and boldness of your plans. You will make me so proud.'

# PART TWO

# The Night Of

Raghu led me out, as his words, 'there is a problem,' echoed in my head. What problem? What could possibly have happened?

We stepped into the elevator, let it sink us into the lobby. Raghu sat in an armchair across from me. He asked someone to bring me coffee and a ham sandwich. I was feeling a little queasy from the alcohol, thanks to Nitya and her damn tequila shots.

'We didn't find Mr. Veitch,' he said, consulting his iPad. 'But we were able to contact his assistant.'

'Oh, right. Ashley.' I said.

'He's gone,' said Raghu, his voice diminished.

'What do you mean he's gone?'

'Ma'am, he's not coming,' he said. 'I have a copy of the contract here. He is within his rights not to come.'

I tore Raghu's iPad out of his thin brown hands. The contract that I had signed glowed in black and white in front of me. Highlighted in neon yellow for my benefit was a paragraph, hidden in the fine print, on page eight.

'Ma'am, according to this, if Applied Automotives is unable to secure the balance of the funding required, then the deal is cancelled. The existing investments are forfeited.'

His eyebrows bristled above his glasses. He looked sterner than I'd ever seen him, not a trace of deference left in his face.

'He told me he had all the money he needed,' I said weakly.

'Were the funds sent to an escrow account?' he asked.

'What's that?'

His sigh could have been heard in Colaba. 'It's a special account, managed by a third party, a place to hold funds until a transaction can be completed.'

'Oh,' I said thickly. Surely, this was Business 101. Surely any business management undergrad at any college in the world or any half-witted intern at any corporation would know this.

The elevator doors opened. My parents and Nitya rushed out. Raghu stood up, went to talk to my father, while my mother sat on the arm of the chair I occupied and held my hand. The two men conversed quietly for a few minutes, and my father looked over at me. The look on his face – disappointment suffused with sadness, overlaid with anger – made me want to cry even more. I knew my father; he wouldn't be mad at me. He would be mad at the man who had done this to me. But that didn't matter. It would have been easier if he had been angry with me. I had been screwed over. Martin Veitch had stolen my father's twelve million dollars, had disappeared and was now taking refuge behind a contract that I had signed.

The elevator opened again, this time allowing Baba and Dadi to step out. Baba joined my father and Raghu, the three of them consulting the iPad, then simultaneously turning to look at me.

Baba walked up to me. 'If you wanted to show me something, you could have come to the house,' he said sternly. 'What was the need for all this nonsense ... cocktails and snacks? What are you trying to prove? And see, still you made a mess.'

I collapsed in tears. Dadi came up behind him, patted my shoulder and followed Baba out of the hotel.

A movement at the entrance distracted me. I turned to look. There stood Bharat, panting as if he'd just run ten miles. I shook my head in his direction, warning him not to come over. I didn't need his advice, his sympathy or whatever it was he was planning on giving me. The colour drained out of his face. He mouthed the words, 'I'm sorry,' a pained expression in his eyes. It was the last thing I saw before my mother gathered me up and took me out to our waiting car, brushing right by him.

# EIGHTEEN

Armaan was back. His flight had landed late from Warsaw. He was on his way to Dome, when my parents had called him and said it was better he not come, to meet us at home instead. I bitterly wondered what business he was up to when not perambulating through Lazienki Park, poking around the Palace on the Island, he and his bloody Ekta, selecting flavours from a Lody stand, sharing platters of pierogis.

I was in my pajamas now, the only clothing option to resort to when your life has gone to hell. The make-up was wiped off, the bright red Valentino gown tossed on the floor. Chanoo would pick it up later, dust it off, hang it up. I never wanted to see it again.

Rajan sat with us. He had not been allowed to come to Dome tonight, my parents insisting he was too young. It was a smart decision. The last thing I needed was my fourteen-year-old brother, the one person in the family who I could reliably count on to look up to me, to see me fail.

My head was in my hands. On my wrists, I could still smell the Lorenzo Villoresi fragrance that the Florentine perfumier had especially concocted for me. It had come in a midnight blue crystal bottle, and he had said that that was me distilled in there – ambitious, strong but still feminine.

Tonight, I felt none of those things.

'What's happening here?' Armaan asked. Leaving his bags in a puddle on the floor at the doorway, he strode into the living room.

My father relayed the incidents of the evening while I sat silently.

My mother, being my mother, figured the thing I needed the most right now was a warm nan kathai and a cup of tea, because in her view of the world, few wrongs couldn't be righted with just the right type of sweet and a bit of chai. Even twelve million dollars worth of wrongs.

It broke my heart that I had lured my beloved Matunga Dada out of the house, for this. I had gone to see him a few days ago, had asked him to come. He had pulled me onto the couch next to him and I had told him of my plan, pleading that the only real blessing I needed was to have him there with me. And he had travelled across town alone, in an auto rickshaw, the exhaust fumes from surrounding traffic thick on his decades-old, frayed suit.

I realized now, far too belatedly, that I had left without saying goodbye to him, that my parents had ushered me out of the lobby before I'd even had a chance to go back up, that Dada would have waited for me alone in a corner of Dome, a space that he would never ever, in his wildest dreams, have imagined could exist in his vision of Bombay.

'Why didn't you come to one of us for advice?' my father asked, looking at me now.

'I wanted to do it all on my own,' I said, tearfully. 'I was scared you would try and talk me out of it.'

'Obviously someone should have,' said Armaan.

'Shut up,' I said. 'You're just jealous. You've been so obsessed with that horrid girlfriend you haven't done a damn thing.'

My brother glared at me, and looked away.

'Stop. Both of you,' my mother said. 'Come, it's late.' It was her common refrain. To her, it was late when things got uncomfortable, truths spoken, lies revealed. She thought it best to retreat behind closed doors, to let calmer heads prevail with daybreak.

Armaan, twenty-eight, six-foot something, about to marry a supermodel, still listened when his mamma told him it was time for bed. He wasn't done making me feel bad, that much I could see. My father, though, stood up, came over to me, put his hand on my shoulder.

'Don't worry Beta,' he said. 'On Monday, I will call the lawyer.' That gave me no hope. I knew better than to trust our broken judicial system, filled with crooked cops and judges amenable to packets of cash to determine which way they should rule. 'We will try and fix it. It was a mistake. Now come, sleep.'

Lights were switched off, plates swept onto trays, faucets turned on in bathrooms as teeth were brushed, faces washed. I walked past my parents' bedroom, on the way to my own. Their door was ajar. I stopped, leaned against the wall, peering in through the crack in the door. My mother sat at her dressing table, smoothening cream onto her hands. My father was perched on the edge of the bed.

'I was wrong to give her the money,' my father said.

'It's what any good father would have done, if he could,' said my mother.

'Yes,' said my father, crossing his ankle over his knee to peel off his socks. 'But in this case, I was mistaken. Because in the end, she has proven herself to be an unworthy and stupid girl.'

I ran down the hallway to my room and quietly shut the door, waiting for the latch to click until I could let myself cry.

# NINETEEN

In the morning, my eyes bleary and head foggy after a restless night, I checked my phone. Nitya had been its caretaker all of yesterday evening. There were fourteen missed calls from Bharat and several texts, each one asking me to stall my announcement till he got there.

At that very second, he called, telling me we needed to meet.

There is a particular slab of concrete above the rocks on Marine Drive that I have secretly claimed as mine. There is nothing to distinguish it from the rest of the raised cement on which lovers nestle, children gingerly skip and old men stop to rest their tired haunches. It is cold and grainy and worn to the touch but there is something in the angle at which it sits when the sun sets, when a particularly buoyant wave hits and a spray of salt leaps up and lands on my lips, that feels comforting to me. Like walking into someone's home for the first time and intuiting where to sit, I had been drawn to this spot years ago, and whenever I was on Marine Drive and it was unoccupied, it is where I would perch.

It was vacant and I was grateful for it. I had told Bharat where to find me and now he eased down next to me. A trio of red pencil-thin marks were stenciled right below his neck. Our legs dangled over the edge facing the ocean. I kicked my right leg up and down slowly like a child.

It was odd seeing him here. His natural habitat seemed to be smoky bars and trendy restaurants and that soulless shell of a place he called home. Not out in the open, in the middle of nature – or as much nature as can be found in South Bombay. He looked milder, like the sea breeze had tamed him.

'It's my fault,' he said, 'that your dad lost eleven-million dollars.'

'Twelve,' I corrected him.

He rubbed his palms against his eyes. When he let go, his eyelashes were pressed together. 'Tania and I were supposed to meet at Dome,' he started.

She had called him from the cab, saying she was twenty minutes from his flat and that she was coming by to pick him up. She showed up early and came upstairs while he was still getting dressed. He felt intruded; he didn't want to go with her in the first place and now he didn't want to be rushed. They started arguing and she lost her temper.

'You don't want to miss the fireworks,' she said. 'That bitch is going to get what she deserves tonight.'

He stopped buttoning his shirt, turned to her. 'What did you do?' he asked.

'Nothing,' she said, suddenly needing to restore civility to the room, equilibrium to the relationship.

He grabbed her upper arm in a tight grip and shook her. 'What did you do?' he asked again.

'That American wanted to cheat her,' she spat the words out. 'I let him.' Tania had thought me an imbecile for not noticing the caveat in the contract, hidden in the fine print. The language was clear enough and I didn't need a law degree from Yale, like she had, to see that Martin Veitch had never had any intention of following through.

'You really are a bitch, you know that?' he said, grabbing his keys off the dining table. He dashed out the front door, letting it slam behind him, leaving Tania inside. He pressed the lift button like a maniac, calling me on his phone simultaneously. The elevator took its time, so he turned to the stairs, bounding down, two at a time. He ran outside the building, yelling at the doorman to fetch him a cab. Tania appeared behind him, stepping out of the lift and running to his side. The cab pulled into the front of the building and Tania elbowed Bharat out of the way to get into it first. When he stopped her, she scratched him. He turned to stare at her, one leg inside the cab, its driver fascinated by what was happening.

'This ends now,' he said to her. 'We're done. Go home.' He slammed the taxi door, leaving her standing there.

By the time he arrived at to Dome, it was too late. I had already made a fool of myself in front of my family.

Now, Bharat looked down at the rocks beneath him for a moment, their surfaces slick with salt water, and then back up, staring out into the horizon. The sky had turned a shade of golden rose, illuminating my slab of concrete.

'I don't get it,' I said. 'Why would she do something like that?'

'She knows I'm into you,' he said, dropping his voice. 'And it made her crazy.'

I thought of his mad dash to me the previous night and the crestfallen look on his face when he saw me. He was gallant and audacious and intrepid.

I sat close to him and let his story unfold.

# TWENTY

I called Matunga Dada the following afternoon. The line crackled. I could imagine him, sitting on his old chair, the leather on its arms worn out by years of use, his gaunt hand clutching the handset of the olive-green rotary dial phone that I was amazed still worked.

'I need to see you,' I said into the phone.

'Then come and see me,' he said.

As I sat alone in the back, I resolved that when I got home that day, I would phone Milan and force him to talk to me. This had gone on too long. Sure, he might have felt that I had betrayed him and the family. But I had just had the most humiliating night of my life. I'd say that that was payback enough.

We ended up driving a little past Matunga Dada's building to avoid a gaping ditch that would screw up traffic on this street for the better part of the month. I imagined poor Dada walking unsteadily down the rickety stairs and out onto this cratered street, having to navigate his way around the boulder-sized cavity in the road as he went on his evening walks, alone. I hated that he was here by himself; my Dada deserved better.

He opened the door to me, a razor in one hand, a snowy mound of shaving cream on his cheek and a threadbare towel thrown over his thin shoulder. 'You have come,' he said, as if I were returning from the dead.

'I said I would, Dada,' I said, grabbing his bony hand, unsure of how to hug him without getting Gillette on my own cheeks.

'Yes, but you young people today say many things,' he smiled.

He led me in, told me to sit while he went into the bathroom to finish up. When he emerged, his face was smooth and clean, marred only by the tiniest little nick beneath his left cheekbone.

'I feel sad about that night,' he said. 'About what happened to you.'

Usually, Dada sat in an armchair across from me. Now, he moved into the space on the couch next to me. He smelled of mint. A tiny tuft of hair curled along his earlobe.

'You don't have to tell me the story,' he said. 'I know what happened. Everyone thinks I am a lonely old man. But I hear everything. This town is full of people eager to share news. Darshan's good friend, Mohan, sometimes comes to the park. He was telling me.'

Every Sunday, Matunga Dada boarded an auto-rickshaw and headed for Shivaji Park where he would congregate with other men like him; elderly, some also widowers, all with too much time on their hands. They were fresh from their afternoon naps, perked up by a hot cup of tea and chai-soaked biscuits and they would walk together until the sun set. In those few hours, Dada heard everything – whose company was on the verge of insolvency, who had succumbed to liver cancer, who was having trouble marrying off a wayward daughter. For a retired group, these men were astonishingly well-connected. Dada had told me once that he would hear things on his weekly sessions with his friends about his own brother, his own family, that he otherwise didn't know. Those men, with their canes, clad in breezy kurtas and bright white sneakers and NYU baseball caps sent by grandsons to shield their scant-haired heads from the fury of the afternoon sun, were their own chat room, their own vibrant, pulsating network when the rest of society had stopped noticing them.

'You don't know the whole truth, Dada,' I said.

Yes, there was a crucial portion of the contract I had foolishly overlooked. But few people were aware that all of it could have been avoided were it not for a screwed-up girl who wanted to get back at me for inadvertently becoming the object of her ex-boyfriend's affection. It was so preposterous, I wouldn't have believed it if it hadn't happened to me – a ridiculous plot twist in one of those daft soap operas people were obsessed with. Messing up on the level that I had, unaided by anyone, was one thing; I couldn't even imagine how derided I would be if it became known that I had entrusted a twelve million dollar deal to someone I didn't know and who had every reason to hate me. I had walked right into it and I had nobody to blame but myself.

But right now, sitting next to my gentle and loving great-uncle, I also needed to unburden myself. He would understand. He would not judge me.

After I told him everything, the whole, unfiltered truth, he laced his long fingers together.

'Is he worthy of you?'

'Ji?' I asked, confused. 'Who?'

'The young man. Is he worthy of all the pain that has been caused to you?'

This was not a question I had asked myself. But when the words came out of Dada's mouth, it became something I was forced to confront. Dada waited for my response, his eyes large and thoughtful behind his glasses.

After what had happened, there was a newfound closeness between Bharat and me. I wasn't the only one who had been wronged; Tania had betrayed him too, even more of a travesty given that she had once claimed to love him. He knew he was foolish to have trusted her, but he genuinely believed they were finally on an even keel, that the jagged edges of their relationship had smoothed out, that they were, finally, 'friends'. And because he felt responsible for what had happened, he had become protective of me.

But the truth was that romantic love, in its first blush, should exist on a continuum; you long to see the person, savour the time together, are left with a warm glow after the encounter is over, can't wait for it to happen again.

So far, I did not have this with Bharat. He did not whisper Rumi to me in the dead of night. He did not come rushing to my side when I ached for comfort. Our encounters seemed to live in a compartment of their own, leaving me with neither anticipation nor longing, their nuances not bleeding into other areas of my life, as love does, when love is true.

'You hesitate,' Dada said. 'The love, it isn't there yet.'

The muffled chime of the doorbell sounded. The focus shifted away from me and I was relieved. Dada's servant scurried to the door. I heard a shuffle of footsteps, a familiar voice.

Milan entered the hall, approached Dada, bowed down and touched our great-uncle's feet. He was not expecting to see me.

'Sit,' Dada said, making room for Milan on the other side of him. 'I am glad you have come.'

It was like a scene from a bad romantic comedy, where an interested onlooker tries to reunite two feuding lovers. Dada had set us up.

'Now, my children,' Dada said. A clock ticked loudly on the wall behind us. Tea and cold glasses of water were brought in.

Dada placed one hand on my knee, the other on Milan's. 'I am going to tell you a story.'

There was a big Diwali party, he said, two decades ago, at Baba's house.

'All the children were playing outside in the garden, so many boys, the friends of all the grandsons. I had brought a big orange ball and I threw it high up in the air, and everyone jumped for it. There were only three little girls playing. You, Sohana, were one of them.'

As he spoke, I cast my memory back. I remembered that day. I was six years old, and I could still, now, smell the new rubber of the ball, feel the powdery dust it left on my fingertips.

'The game turned ugly,' Dada said, his voice softening. 'They made it boys against girls. The two other girls ran off, their chotis flying behind them. You, Sohana. You stayed.'

The boys, my cousins and their friends, decided to take turns throwing the ball at me, to see who could swipe me with it the most times.

'You were crying, Sohana. But you stayed. When even Armaan, your own brother, started to hit you with the ball, I came running out.'

Milan, then a cheeky eight-year-old, had stood up to defend me. He shielded me behind spread-eagled arms and when the others – his brother, mine, two older and more menacing cousins – commanded him to back off, he told them the only way they would get to me was through him. I cowered behind him until we were called in to eat.

I looked at Milan now, who was staring at a spot on the patterned rug, between his feet. I could hear him breathing.

'Forgive an old man's long stories,' said Dada. 'But when I think of you children, that's the one day I remember the most. Because it was the day when I saw who the two of you really are and what you would always be to one another.'

A tear trickled down my cheek. Dada put his arm around me, pulled me in to him. 'You are not the only Badshah to come and see me,' he said. 'Preeti calls me regularly. She's a blessing to the family, that one. It has upset her no end that you two are not speaking. Sohana, Beti, you are the only one who been able to control this wild cousin of yours. And you, Milan, you understand Sohana better than anyone. You should be working together. Not fighting. Please.'

I had never before seen Milan look ashamed.

'Mother Nature is calling,' Dada said, standing up. 'You two, talk.'

He quietly left the room.

'This whole friggin' thing is a mess, man,' Milan said. 'I got so damned pissed off with you for talking to the press, making everything worse. And then going and doing your own thing without saying anything to me.'

'I tried to talk to you,' I said. 'You didn't want to hear it.'

'I'm sorry all that shit happened,' he said. 'That you lost all that money.'

'It's okay,' I said. 'I'll survive. But what's going on with you?' I asked him. 'I'm working on a couple of things,' he said. He looked away, out the window.

'It's okay. You don't have to tell me.'

'It's not that. Just don't want to jinx it. Anushka keeps reminding me that it's best not to say anything until it's finalized. It's how she approaches her film career. I want to do the same.'

'She's smart,' I said. 'So things are going well between the two of you?'

A soft smile rolled across his face.

'She's amazing,' he said. 'She's in Mauritius, shooting. But I'm going to propose to her when she gets back. I'm going to beat that bloody brother of yours to the mandap and to the head of the company too.'

'I have no doubt,' I said. This was what I had missed; Milan's bluster, his bravado.

Dada returned, drops of water sprinkled on the front of his kurta, his hands still moist from washing them. He smiled when he saw Milan and I talking, our bodies relaxed, facing one another on his threadbare couch. He said he needed to nap, it was time for us to leave. Milan held my arm as we walked down the steps, the decaying wood creaking beneath our feet, threatening to crumble.

# TWENTY-ONE

*It has been four days since what happened with Sohana.*

*On that night, when she started speaking, the family quietly listened. There was a fancy screen behind her with pictures of new cars, cars of the future, cars that use water instead of petrol. I cannot imagine such a thing. These young people today, my grandchildren and their friends, they are the ones who want to live in the world of tomorrow. They cannot wait to get there. Me, I prefer the past.*

*But my opinions do not matter. If they did, I would have been asked for them long ago. That night, when my granddaughter first started to explain what she planned to do with this water car, I looked at Baba, at my sons. They looked impressed, surprised even, that this ordinary girl was suddenly using the language of big business and had come up with such grand ideas. I thought maybe this girl will know how to make Badshah look good again.*

*But then Jeetu's man, that skinny, serious chap whose name I cannot remember, whispered something into her ear. I noticed the scared look on her face when he took her off somewhere. I knew then that something had gone wrong.*

*After half an hour, the screen was taken down, all that equipment put away in steel cases. The girl was in the middle of saying something and suddenly it was finished.*

*Later, I heard what had happened … that the man in America had cheated her. Baba was so mad. It wasn't just because money had disappeared; my husband has lost much more than that in his years, he too has made mistakes. But he was mad that his granddaughter allowed someone to cheat her so easily. It made him angry to think that that man must be off somewhere, laughing about how he has made a fool of the Badshahs. Nothing makes Baba angrier than that.*

*But right now, I don't want to think about any of that. Right now, I just want to smile and remember how nice it was to see Ram, my dear brother-in-law, who had come to the party that night. I hardly see him, so sometimes in my mind, I think of him the way the rest of my family does, as Matunga Dada, as if he is known to me only because that's where he lives.*

*I saw him that night, looking thin and small on one of those big white sofas, being looked after by Preeti, may Krishna bless her for her kindness. I had not seen him out of his house since Sharan and*

*Jaanvi's wedding. His suit no longer fits him. I went up to say hello to him. He's my brother-in-law after all, my only one too.*

*Baba remained where he was. Five decades and the hate remains.*

*Ram was happy to see me. He put his arm around my shoulder and I lightly touched the back of his jacket, an awkward hug, despite the happiness that shone in his eyes. His clothes smelled musty. I picked up the faint whiff of 4711, from a bottle he must surely have had for many years.*

*How different an embrace it was from the very first time.*

# TWENTY-TWO

I had fallen prey to a condition I was rarely susceptible to: envy.

I had never had reason to experience it; people were jealous of me, not the other way around. To them, I had everything and I had never desired the things I didn't have – husband, kids, a home of my own; I figured those would eventually come along.

But now, I did start to begrudge other young women their success; I would read stories of brilliant women in their Silicone Valley start-ups, their genius ideas for this product and that, how they scaled the corporate ladder at quicksilver speed. I couldn't even make excuses for why they had succeeded and I hadn't, couldn't attribute their ascent to family connections or money. I had had all of those things too, had every advantage.

I just had to face the fact that everyone else was smarter and luckier than me. It did not help that I was feeling ex-communicated by my family. My parents changed the subject every time I walked into a room; I know they would have been talking about what had happened, but they didn't feel the need to include me in the conversation, as if I had had nothing to do with it, as if I was a child unable to handle the truth. They had tried to comfort me initially, it was okay, we all make mistakes. But I could tell they didn't really mean it. My father, especially, looked at me with such sore disappointment that there were moments I couldn't bear to return his gaze. I wished they would just say it; tell me I was a fool, tell me they never should have trusted me.

Jag Skyped me, the first time in a long time. I didn't bother prettying myself up for the video chat. I had fallen into a depression and the last thing that depressives care about is whether their lipstick matches their eyeshadow.

'What next?' he asked, his face earnest. A tall glass of beet and apple juice was to the left of his laptop, his early morning staple.

'I'm thinking a bit of revenge might be called for,' I said. 'That Tania chick screwed me over. My uncle, Amit, knows some shady people who will know how to dispose of a body. Chainsaws are cheaply available here, you know.'

'Sohana Badshah, Assassin.' Jag smiled.

'So, why did she do it?' he asked.

I remembered the floral nightgown on the armchair in his bedroom, the pink batik toiletry bag. Jag had moved on. It was time he knew that I had, too.

'She was jealous,' I said.

'Of what?'

'Him and me.'

It took him a few seconds to process that chip of information and then it seemed to hit him like a hard slap to the face.

'Oh,' he said. 'Wow.'

He stared at me though the thirteen-inch screen, his face condensed, his voice muted and he seemed frail for a second, reduced. In that second, I saw that I still meant something to him, even if he had someone else, that there was a part of him still connected to me and, with a few short words, I had just severed it.

'You guys are dating?'

'Sort of,' I said.

'Wow,' Jag said again,

'What?'

'He just doesn't seem your type.'

'And who is? You?' Talking to him now, given the way I had been feeling, was not a good idea. I was irritated and needed to take it out on someone.

'I was in college with him for four years,' Jag said. 'I know him better than you do.' He paused. 'Just be careful. Okay?'

There it was. Jag trying to save me. Jag trying to protect me. I was infuriated. I had messed up on a business deal. Jag would never say so, but he must have thought me obtuse in the extreme. And now, here he was, warning me away from any romantic inclinations I might have towards a man he had introduced me to, a man who had, indirectly, created the mess in which I found myself. I felt cornered, belittled.

'You know Jag, why is it okay for you to have found someone else and me to not?'

A puzzled look crossed his face. 'What are you talking about?' he asked.

'When you showed me your flat that time, I saw women's stuff. In your bedroom.'

There was an accusing tone in my voice that had no business being there.

'I have no idea what you're going on about,' he said. 'What women's stuff?' Then, a second of clarity. 'Oh, that,' he said. 'My sister was visiting. I gave her my room.'

I wanted a sinkhole to open up beneath me and swallow me whole. I felt such a fool. Firstly for bringing it up – whether Jag had a serious girlfriend or a one-night-stand – it was none of my business. We were over. And then I'd gone and thrown out the idea that I was with someone new because he was! It felt juvenile, like I was in the middle of some soppy teenage drama. I needed to get offline before things got worse. I told him I had to go and disconnected abruptly.

I was on edge for another reason. It was Friday night. Dinner at Baba's. The first family gathering since The Night Of. I felt sick.

# TWENTY-THREE

*I'm usually grateful when the Friday family dinner is over, so I can take off my sari, sprinkle some Johnson's Baby Powder on my legs, put on my cotton nightdress and relax with some tea, without having to talk anymore or listen to anyone.*

*Tonight, I was glad to see the last person walk out through the door, into the waiting car that would take them to their own home, their own problems. I don't need them to be bringing their worries into my life. Yes, they are my family. They are my sons, my daughters-in-law, my grandchildren. I am allowed, as the Badshah family dadi, to play favourites, aren't I? It should be one of the few small rewards I have earned, having been married to this man all these many years, to have given him three sons, to have arranged wasteful weddings and blessed selfish grandsons. It is said that there is no end to a mother's love. That is true. But there can be an end to a mother's patience, to her goodwill.*

*Tonight, I was surprised to see Sohana. I would not have blamed her if she had wanted to stay home, after what happened last week. If I were her, I may not have wanted to show my face in public for some time. She made me proud by coming tonight. She has rarely missed a family Friday dinner and her presence is always a pleasure. Baba especially has always loved to see her; she is happy and easygoing and full of light conversation that threatens no one. It was good that she could swallow her pride and come over.*

*Sometimes, when I have a free evening, I sit and watch an American movie on TV. I especially like the dramas, with lots of talking. I much prefer them to the bang-bang-boom-boom movies, guns and shooting. Baba enjoys those, but they give me a headache.*

*What I like about the American movies is how open people are, how they talk about difficult things. They sit around a dinner table and there can be tears and shouting, slamming doors and people leaving, but, later, hugs are given, confessions made, love expressed. Of course, I know they are just actors and actresses playing a part on a screen, but I think that this is how things are for other families; that anger can be shown and then people can talk and unite again.*

*With all we have – the money, the name, the status – why can my family not do this?*

*That was what I was thinking when Sohana walked through the door tonight, looking shy and scared. During drinks and appetizers, she stayed close to her mother, like a child among strangers, only speaking quietly to Jaanvi and Preeti. When Milan arrived, he went and talked to her. I was happy to see that; I know there had been some trouble between them. After Baba and I are gone from this world, and our sons have no need to be nice to one another anymore and the family will fall apart over money, I believe that Sohana and Milan would stay close for the rest of their lives, their own children playing together like they themselves used to.*

*We took our regular places around the dinner table, Baba on his tall lion chair, the rest of us scattered around him. Armaan had brought Ekta, that fancy girl he wants to be engaged to. She hogged all the limelight. Ekta is a fashion model of the worst kind. It is one thing that she is taller than all of us, it is not her fault that she was born with those giraffe legs, but she has learnt how to look down at people, as if we are not worth being in her sight. She is especially nice to Baba, knowing that he holds the key to her boyfriend's fortune. She cares nothing for Jeetu and Asha and less for me, as I am to her only the old lady in the nice sari, the quiet one sitting at Baba's elbow. She will stare at my jewellery and then she will look away.*

*At the dinner table, taking one hour to eat a small pakoda, she talked non-stop about her shoots. She had gone to Paris for a fashion show, went to a fancy party afterwards, was introduced to some famous singer, some Ree-Hannah. For twenty minutes, Ekta told us about their conversation, what she wore, the photographers, that she came in all the French magazines. I tried to drop her a hint, that she should stop talking, by offering her more food but she ignored me, and kept on talking, Baba glaring at her with each word. People like Ekta think that just because a family is rich rich rich, they are also modern and free-thinking. Some families are. Mine is not. It was hard enough for Baba to accept that one of his grandsons wants to marry a girl who tries on clothes for a living, posing in front of cameras with her breasts hanging out. Why the silly girl felt the need to keep talking on about it in front of him, made no sense to me. Armaan finally made her shut up by pointing out Malini's new Bulgari watch and Ekta said how much she would like the same one, and then she stopped talking.*

*I noticed Sohana eating her dal and mutton biryani quietly. The girl has become so thin, I wished someone – Baba, one of my sons, a grandson even – had said something, had asked her how she was feeling, reassured her that it was okay that she was cheated, that it happens, that there is nothing to feel bad about. Even if they were to lie to her, they should have said something.*

*But nobody did. Not even I.*

*When I look at the magazines while sitting at the beauty parlour, I read all about famous, beautiful people who have everything and are loved by many. They are worshipped and adored by strangers. But it is those closest to these celebrities who know the truth, who must want to shout to the world: 'you can't imagine how truly terrible this person is, how selfish, how mean. You would never want a friend like this.'*

*I thought of that this evening, as we sat around the table at dinner, all of us avoiding the pain of one of our own, right in front of us. I thought of how everyone in Bombay wants to be friends with the Badshahs, they want to boast about coming to one of our parties. But they don't know that, behind the whiskey and diamonds, most of us are nothing, that we have not yet learnt how to speak to one another in a kind way, that an uncle cannot take a niece aside and offer her some consolation, that there is so much anger here, right at this table, that it poisons the air we breathe.*

*I understand the need for silence; for Amit or Prakash or Jeetu or Baba to open the conversation about what has happened to Sohana, they would have to start talking about the reason it happened, which would mean talking about Baba's decision. So far, nobody wants to talk about that. Newspaper articles are written, our friends gossip, and here, in our own households, nothing is discussed between father and sons, brother and brother.*

*Baba made that decision months ago, to make his grandsons fight over his company. Before he made it, he talked to nobody, not even me. The night he made his announcement, I told him, when we came home, that he was making a mistake. He was sitting on a chair, untying his shoelaces. He told me it was not my concern, that I didn't know anything, that I should stay out of it and then he let out a big belch and went into the bathroom.*

*A few years ago, when I was looking through the TV channels for Zee Jagran, I stumbled across some educational program about animals. I am not interested in those nature programs but the American lady was talking about big bears – grizzlies, they are called. She said that the male grizzly killed his own cubs for food, that the only enemy he would meet would be the mother bear, who would fight him to the death to protect her babies. For a long time, I haven't thought of that image – of a massive, hairy creature tearing apart his own small babies..*

*But tonight, after everyone left, my sons broken, my grandsons anxious and Baba had gone upstairs in one of the bad moods he is in so often these days, I remembered the grizzly bear and I saw the same thing happening here, in my own house; my husband is killing his own children.*

*I have to fight to protect them.*

# TWENTY-FOUR

I realized, in the aftermath of what had happened, that I had absolutely nothing to fall back on.

Admittedly, prior to my botched foray into the business world, my life had been shallow, but now it seemed quite drained of any potential. I had been so singularly focused on launching the Vecco – it had quite literally taken over my life – that now I felt as if I were existing in a void.

I had a friend, years ago, who had spent eight months planning her wedding, jetting off to London and New York, Miami and Delhi to shop for her trousseau, planning nine different parties spread between three cities. For those eight months, she couldn't think of anything else.

Then, a month before the wedding, her fiancé was arrested for embezzlement and ended up in jail. She wasn't exactly the stick-by-your-guy-through-thick-and-thin sort of girl anyway, so it was over as soon as he was led off in handcuffs. She was wrecked emotionally – not because she was torn from the man she supposedly loved, but because there seemed to be no purpose to her life anymore. After months of being constantly on-call with caterers and couturiers, her phones were suddenly quiet, the congratulations silenced, deposits forfeited, her life flaccid.

I didn't understand her depression back then. But now, I did. There had been a force propelling me forwards, something to work towards, a life to plan for. And without any warning, it was gone.

One evening, particularly vulnerable, I confided to Bharat my feelings, as we sat at the dining table in his flat, drinking coconut water. I stared at the flecks of white wafting in the opaque liquid. I waited for him to mock me, or ignore me, reactions I still expected from him, even though I had no reason for doing so. He did neither. He listened. I waited for him to put his hand over mine, a small move – a Jag move – that would have consoled me. He didn't.

'Nobody has told me to try again,' I said.

'They wouldn't.'

'Why? Because I would fail a second time?'

'No. Because this has all just happened. It would be like telling someone who is separated to start dating again.' He paused. 'But do you want to? Try again?'

I pushed my chair out, the legs letting out a tiny mewl against the floor. I walked over to the window, sealed off and soundproof. I missed the noisy clamour of the city below, the distraction it provided. In the reflective glass pane, I saw Bharat behind me, still seated at the table, glancing my way.

'I don't think so,' I said. Even to my own ears, I sounded defeated, pitiful. 'I think I'm done with trying to be a woman of big business.'

'What will you do now?' he asked.

'Whatever I was doing before,' I replied. 'Absolutely nothing.'

I realized I was grateful for him. What had happened had brought us closer together, his guilt lowering his defenses, softening his edges. I recalled Jag's words – that Bharat was not my type, his warning to be careful. Careful of what? Falling in love and getting hurt again? I thought it laughable that Jag wanted to protect my feelings, when he himself had so coolly trashed my heart not that long ago. I remembered Jag's face the last time we had spoken, when I had told him about my relationship with Bharat, the disappointment in his eyes. I had thought then that perhaps Jag's reaction was one of jealousy, of sadness, that I had finally found someone else. But it wasn't that. He was questioning my taste, disbelieving that I could fall for a man who was, admittedly, more dispassionate than I'd like, a man who would start building walls again.

But I didn't want to think about any of that now. Bharat stood up, joined me at the window. I could feel his soft breath at my ear, the coarseness of his goatee against my cheek. I let myself sink into the pleasure of it, transient though it may be.

# TWENTY-FIVE

Armaan was hunched over the carom board, his lean, muscular shoulders like powdery ski slopes under a white cotton shirt. He was playing with Rajan, the younger boy whooping every time he flicked a coin into a netted pocket. It had been a while since the two brothers – some 14 years apart in age – had done anything together. I fetched a glass of lime soda from the kitchen and went to join them.

'Didi, I'm epic at this game,' my younger brother said.

'I'm glad to see you playing with something that doesn't have to be plugged in,' I said.

Armaan looked over at me. He arched his back, rubbed the nail of his third finger with his long thumb and prepared to go in for the kill. He aimed at the rose-tinted queen, which went flying off the board.

'Raja, go get some powder,' said Armaan. 'The board is getting rough.'

'Loser,' Rajan teased, before racing off. Knowing him, he would be sidetracked by one of a dozen other things before making his way back here. He was a teenage boy, after all.

The thought of being alone with Armaan made me surprisingly uncomfortable. Things still hadn't healed between us, not really. He got off the floor and sat on the couch next to me.

'How're you doing, Sis?' he asked. 'Life treating you okay?'

'Are you speaking to me?' I asked him.

He snorted gently through his nose as he pulled out a piece of chewing gum from his pocket. 'I realized I needed to get over it,' he said, unwrapping it and putting it in his mouth. 'You made a mistake. Did you ever find out what happened to the bastard? The one who took our money?'

'No. I think daddy and Raghu are trying to deal with it. I just don't have the energy. You know, it was my fault too. I messed up with the contract.'

'Yeah. And he took advantage of that.'

I could see that he was twitching to smoke; his fingers rubbed together, his foot tapped lightly on the carpeted floor – the beginning of a restlessness that would hold sway over him until he got his fix of nicotine. My face reddened.

I needed everyone around me to stop making me feel stupid. There was that well-trod line – nobody can make you feel anything without your permission. Well, as I discovered, it was a patent untruth. People could make you feel all sorts of crap whether you gave them permission to or not.

Armaan moved closer to me on the couch. I willed Rajan to come back in, to alleviate the defensiveness I felt in the presence of my older brother. Armaan put his arm around my shoulder. 'Sorry, Sis,' he said. 'I don't want to make you feel bad. Shit happens. Dad isn't going to go to the poor house over this. We'll all live. You just made a mistake.'

'Thanks, Ba,' I said, resting my head on his shoulder. 'That really means a lot to me.'

He shifted, and I straightened myself. He stood up and stretched. He was off to meet Ekta. While my night was coming to an end, his was just beginning. But this was good. We had talked, had cleared the air. He understood and he didn't blame me.

'Just know your limits, Sis,' he said, turning around to walk out of the room. 'You taking over the family business?' He shook his head and laughed. 'Quit while you're behind.'

## TWENTY-SIX

*The ladies met for rummy today. All the women chattering about this and that, rogan josh recipes (such a joke, as if any of them even cook anymore), whose husband needs dialysis, which is the best tablet for gas. We started to gossip about the latest news in town. Paru, who likes to nose around in everybody's business, mentioned that Ravi Dutta, who was her brother-in-law's nephew on his other side, is my grandson, Karan's business partner.*

*'Who?' I asked. 'What?' I knew of no such partnership.*

*'You didn't know? Karan is partnering with Chandru Dutta's son for some business venture. My husband was saying something about it. Ravi is a good boy.'*

*Ravi Dutta was many things, but a good boy was not one of them. I had loved his mother, Heera. She had passed away – very bad bronchitis – and her husband Chandru, had remarried. His second wife was widowed herself, with a grown son. These stories were like TV serials, playing out around me.*

*After his mother died, Ravi had begun drinking a lot and everyone says he also took drugs. He could not make good decisions at his father's company; he almost lost everything. Chandru asked him to leave and had put Simran, his stepson, in charge. Ravi had gone to New York where he worked with a company that destroyed other companies. I didn't believe what Paru was saying. There was no need for Karan to take a partner, especially a man like Ravi Dutta.*

*Truthfully, I have always worried about Karan and Sharan; they are unstable like their parents. There is gossip that my daughter-in-law Malini, is having an affair with a cricket player, that she's cheating on my son.*

*From the beginning, I knew there would be problems with her. At the engagement dinner, she had insisted on Western dancing; that is okay, I have tried from the beginning to be a modern mother-in-law. There was a DJ, some fat, sweating fool that Malini's parents had found from I-don't-know-where. She wanted her favourite songs played. The DJ put on some idiotic song tune, where the lady wailed and wailed 'call me' a hundred times in the song. Malini was wearing a dark blue sequinned sari, many sapphires around her neck, gifted to her by us. She moved her pallu out of the way and started to move sexily, too too sexily, shaking her bum and stomach, like a belly dancer. She has always had a good figure; even now, with two grown sons, she has managed to keep herself slim. Amit was staring at her as she danced, his tongue hanging out. Everyone was staring. I turned to Baba and I said, 'Does she have no sharam?' He didn't reply, only drank more whisky, his eyes growing redder and sleepier. I blamed him, for he was the one who found Malini for Amit. There were many girls who wanted him. We were already rich then. Not rich like we are now, which is rich beyond rich, but we had plenty of money and the town knew that. Malini was chosen for her beauty … there is no brain in that head of hers and her heart is dirty.*

*At the Datar, immediately after the wedding, she did something I could not forgive. The palmful of sweaty salt passed first between her and Amit, then to Baba, then I, then our other boys, and on through many sleepy small cousins and old women who had taken off their shoes already. I told Ram, my only brother-in-law, 'Bhau, please come, do the datar with the new bahu of the house.' His wife, my bhabi, had gone home. Malini turned to Amit and said, 'Why should I do this with him? He is a nobody.' My blood boiled. I wanted to slap her. She said to me, 'Mummy, I'm very tired now.' And she threw the salt onto the silver tray and left. The look on Ram's face, when it was clear that the newest addition to the family did not respect him, killed me.*

*After Amit and Malini came back from their honeymoon, I went to talk to her. 'I didn't want to say anything to you on your wedding night,' I told her. Her white, pretty face turned serious.*

*'You showed disrespect to Matunga Dada that night. You called him a nobody.'*

*'No, Mummy,' she lied. 'I was just tired, so many people to do the ceremony with. I would never say anything like that.'*

*'All this,' I swept my arm across the room, 'we would have none of it if it wasn't for Baba's brother. From now on, you will show him as much respect as you do to us.'*

*Her eyes were wide. She looked scared.*

*'Do you understand me?' I said.*

*As I left, she rushed to touch my feet. I lightly put my hand on the top of her head, pretending to bless her.*

*Malini and Amit have had problems as all married couples do. I have learned to let them fight and make up, raise their children the way they choose. Only once did I tell Malini, when Sharan and Karan were small, that her sons were bullies. They treated their younger cousins terribly, Sohana especially. She was the only girl and needed them to be like big brothers to her, not enemies. They pulled her ponytail, kicked her, threw paint down her party dress, laughing as she cried. If a boy cannot treat a sister well, then how will he treat any woman well? Malini told me that Sohana had to learn how to fight for herself, that boys will be boys, it was just children playing. She never understood that children already are what they will become – leaders or followers, thoughtful or selfish, cowards or heroes. Children know who they are, long before their parents do.*

*I hear Malini is not true to my son, that there is another man. They say he is a cricket player, much younger than her. He is a hero. Even I have heard of him, and I do not follow such things. He used to be a drinker, I have read. His bride left him. He was a nobody. Then he stopped drinking, devoted his life to cricket, and see, he became rich and famous. Cricket players are very fashionable right now. They are what movie stars used to be. Everybody wants to go to parties with them, marry them, have affaires with them. The woman who should never have married my son loves another. I must try to understand. I know what it is to live with one man and love another. Decades have passed, how many tears have been shed over it, my bhabi laid to rest on her funeral pyre with a heart filled with sadness that her husband loved another for all of their lives. But we have all survived, have made the most of it. Because of what I know, have been through myself, I must show Malini some understanding.*

# TWENTY-SEVEN

All the cosy, red couches at Coffee Bean were taken, not surprising given that it was a Saturday afternoon and a movie had just finished at the adjacent theater, spilling out dazed people into the mall. Nitya managed to get a table after she ordered a poor chap to leave as he had long ago finished his drink and was sitting alone, his laptop bag and books taking up two other seats.

'Jerk,' Nitya said uncharitably, dusting crumbs off the table, not attempting to disguise the contempt on her face. The young man was barely out of earshot.

'Cool it,' I said. Wherever Nitya went, drama inevitably followed.

We hadn't seen one another in weeks – what with her ascent to the top of the business world and my journey in the opposite direction. She would text me intermittently from Bangalore, Mauritius, Sharjah and was back home for a few days.

Things were going brilliantly for her. She had invested in her cousin's company which distributed famous cosmetics brands in Eastern Europe. She had learnt how to invest in commodities and actually knew what a pork barrel was. A year ago, the girl was borrowing her friends' designer dresses to impress me. Now, she could afford to buy anything she wanted.

'I'm really glad you've done so well,' I said, faking a smile, forcing a cheer in my voice.

'I'm sorry I've not been around much, while you've been going through all this stuff,' she said. How are you? What's been going on?' she asked.

I hadn't yet told her about Bharat. I had wanted to wait until my feelings for him were clearer. But Nitya had sat down and usurped the conversation, had just spent twenty minutes recounting every one of her victories, delineating the opportunities that lay strewn out for her. Bharat was the only thing I did have that was new. It was the only thing I could talk to her about.

'Well, I've met someone,' I said. 'We've been spending time together. I don't know how serious it is yet. But it's good.' I told her about him and how we had met.

'That snobby bearded guy from the sangeet?' she asked, referring to the night she had briefly met him, at Dipo and Kalpana's party. 'He doesn't seem your type.'

'That's what Jag said.'

'Jag knows? That you're fooling around with a guy he introduced you to, to help you in your business? And who kind of caused the failure of it?'

She pushed her coffee cup out of the way.

'Stop,' I said. 'Don't judge me, please. This is just something I need right now.'

'Okay,' she said. 'I'm sorry I called him snobby. You owe it to yourself to have a little fun. As long as he's worthy of you.'

The concern in her eyes made me cry.

'What's going on with you, Soh,' she asked, leaning over more closely.

I pulled a tissue out of handbag and loudly blew my nose.

'Look, you tried something and it didn't work out,' she continued. 'You can't just give up. All the greatest businesspeople in history – do you think success came to them on the first try? You can't be so defeated, Soh. You will survive this.'

'That's easy for you to say,' I said. 'Things are going so great for you.' I hated admitting it, even to myself, but I was a little jealous of her. Ironic, really, given that it wasn't that long ago that she had harboured the same feelings towards me, but we had cleared the air and had become closer.

'Yes, but I've had my down times too. You remember. I had nothing.'

I nodded. I just wanted to shake this off – the self-loathing, the general malaise I felt. I wanted to be happy again.

'I have an idea,' said Nitya. 'Why don't you and I do something together?'

'What do you mean?'

'In business. As partners. I'm sort of getting the hang of it. I'll tell you what I'm working on and we can do it together. It will be great fun!'

I appreciated Nitya's cheerleading approach, the generosity of her gesture. But it felt forced to me, something she was moved to do because she felt she owed me something.

'Thanks, Nits,' I said. 'I'll figure something out.'

She looked past my shoulder. I turned to follow her gaze and saw Milan walk in, uncharacteristically early for our meeting. He was followed, surprisingly, by Pawan.

'I'll take your leave,' she said, gathering her things. 'We can talk another time. Just promise me you'll think about it. Okay?'

She brushed past my cousins on the way out and they exchanged tepid smiles.

'How's Madam?' Milan asked, taking Nitya's vacated seat.

'Being very sweet, actually,' I said.

Pawan leaned down to kiss me. There was something in his face that was comforting; he had begun to resemble Matunga Dada; the same slender, serious face, a peaceful detachment in his demeanour, eyes that rested kindly behind his glasses. I was surprised I'd never noticed the similarities before.

'We've teamed up,' Milan said, his elbow resting on his brother's arm.

'Really?' I said. 'That's great. On what?'

The last time Milan and I had talked about what he had planned to do, he was looking at a photosynthesis microchip, something Jag had turned me on to.

'We're not doing that,' Milan added, reading my mind. 'Pawan has the brains in this operation and we're going to use them.'

I looked over at my introverted other cousin, whose humble exterior belied the enormity of his intellect. When all this had started, he had said something about military drones, as a way to inveigle the Badshahs with the Ministry of

Defence. All that had sounded a bit too hard-core for me. I was hoping he'd had a change of heart.

'I was looking at an ad for a jeans brand,' said Pawan, his tone staccato, his voice low.

'What?' I said, startled.

'Just listen,' Milan cut in, putting his hand on my sleeve.

'So I was looking at these jeans and the model was wearing them with a white T-shirt. And underneath, it said, 'Back to Basics'. And I thought, 'that's it'!'

'What's it?' I asked.

'That. Back to basics,' he said, unhelpfully.

'Steel,' Milan clarified. 'What we show Baba. It will be in steel. The new direction he wants to take the company in. It will be based on the old. Baba thinks he wants change. He doesn't. He wants more of the same. Just better. My brother is going to give that to him.'

As my cousins talked, a veil around my head lifted. The fog cleared. The boys were right. I was amazed that nobody else seemed to have seen it. Baba had started with a steel mill, all those many decades ago. So much else followed – hotels and petrochemicals and real estate and technology and things small and large that I would never fully know. But he loved steel – the purification of the raw iron, the inclusion of the elements, the fury of the fire. His sweat had dripped onto sheets and strappings and tubes. He had a kinship with the hard, cold material that was his own. As my cousins talked, I knew one thing to be true; they were onto something.

# TWENTY-EIGHT

It was week three and Mary was growing weary. She didn't think she could make it through another six weeks of this. Immediately after the end of the chanting of the Novenas today, she had made her way to the priest and had expressed her frustration. She told him she had initially been confident that The Lady of Perpetual Succour would begin the granting of her wish. But that, a third of the way into it, progress had certainly been slow.

'My child, God's plans require patience,' said Father Joseph, a weathered man with whiskery eyebrows.

'I don't have time for patience,' Mary said. Earlier, she had looked at the pious people around her, so filled with faith and devotion, so sure that their prayers would be answered. She wished she shared the same conviction.

'What is it you seek?' he asked.

'The man I love,' she said. 'I want him to return my love.'

'Don't worry too much,' Father Joseph said, patting Mary on her hand, like she was a child who had spilled a glass of juice. He started walking away. 'The best things in life are worth waiting for. I will pray for you.'

Mary willed Father's Joseph's words to make her feel better, but they did not. In the past three weeks, she had construed every spike in Sharan's interest in her as a blessing from the heavens.

In fact, up until just this morning, she had been optimistic. The previous evening, instead of meeting Sharan in a hotel room after work like they usually did, she had been caught by surprise by a chartered helicopter ride over the city. He had clutched her hand and pointed out Filmcity and Essel World, told stories about an unimaginably tacky wedding he had been to at the first and how he had once taken Rajan, his youngest cousin, to the second. Mary had let his words waft in the air around her, not really taking them in, instead sinking into the spontaneity of the moment, to gloat over the fact that her elusive, married, distracted boss-lover had thought of her, had bothered to call somebody and make a plan that would elevate her, quite literally, from her life. She had floated home, freshly convinced of his love for her.

But this morning, Mary finally plummeted back to earth. She had answered Sharan's phone on his desk before he arrived at work. It was his friend, Tushar.

'Can you give him a message?' Tushar asked.

'Of course, Sir,' said Mary, still ecstatic, pulling out her notepad.

'Please tell him we're sorry that we didn't make the helicopter ride at the last minute. My wife got sick. We'd like to thank Jaanvi for arranging it. I hope he got rid of the tickets.'

Mary felt like an invisible hand had swiped through the air and slapped her on the face. It had never been meant for her; that trip through the stars, champagne in the clouds, his whispers of nostalgia at a thousand feet high. She had been there by default.

When Sharan arrived at the office, Mary was uncommonly cold to him.

'What? You got your period or something?' Sharan asked her, grumpily. The magic of last night evaporated, as she thumped down his morning tea on his desk a little too forcefully, sending sweet brown drops over the rim of the cup and onto the plate. She ignored him the rest of the day.

Now, she left the church, started to walk home, pushing through the evening crowds that gathered around paan stalls and loitered on the sidewalk smoking beedis.

She thought of Father Joseph's words again. Maybe he was right. She remembered something she had read in an old copy of Reader's Digest at the doctor's office. 'Infinite patience produces immediate results.' She didn't understand that back then – it had seemed almost counter-intuitive. How could endlessly waiting for something to happen, make it happen?

But she could see a sliver of truth to it. It was the same resoluteness, the absence of anxiety that she had witnessed in the people around her tonight. It was like they just knew that something would be so. For her, that meant having faith that Sharan would eventually find his way to her. It meant trusting the outcome, not obsessing over the process. It meant just sticking this out for six more weeks and waiting for the miracle.

Now, in the calm aftermath of her time at church, she felt bad about how she had treated Sharan this morning. After all, even if he hadn't planned the helicopter adventure with her in mind, he had still taken her. He could have cancelled the whole thing. Or, worse still, taken his wife. He did mean well. She just had to trust him.

As she neared the street to her parent's flat, she dug into her bag for her phone. She needed to hear Sharan's voice and clear the air about her rudeness today. She dialled his mobile. It rang four times and went to voicemail. She didn't bother leaving a message, and started to put her phone away. It rang, Sharan's number showing up on her caller ID.

'Hi baby,' she purred. 'I miss you.'

'Who is this?' said a woman's voice.

'Oh, shit,' said Mary, stunned. She stopped walking, let the crowds shove past her.

'Who am I talking to?' the woman asked again.

'Wrong number,' Mary mumbled and hung up on her boss's wife.

Immediately, her phone rang again. She switched it off and shoved it deep inside her bag, as if to bury it forever.

'What the hell were you thinking?' Sharan raged in the morning, slamming the door to his office behind them.

'I thought you were calling me back,' Mary explained, on the verge of tears. 'How did I know it would be your wife?'

There had been times when she would grow impatient with Sharan and his selfishness, feeling that this whole thing was a mistake, that she deserved better. But when he glared at her like this, fury in his eyes, she shrank. She was terrified that he would toss her out of his life, that she had become more trouble than she was worth.

'She fought with me the whole night,' he said. Outside, rain fell in thick, grey drops, hitting the window heavily. The skies misted over. Mary felt a chill.

Sharan rubbed his hand on his forehead. Mary wanted to reach out and stroke the back of his neck, but Sharan's demeanour told her he didn't want to be touched right now.

'What did you say to her?' Mary asked quietly. She wanted to take the attention away from her stupid, stupid mistake – understandable though it may be, it was still stupid. She wanted Sharan to stop blaming her.

'I couldn't tell her the truth, could I?' he snapped.

'Actually, maybe you could have,' Mary said quietly.

'Are you nuts?' he yelled.

She stiffened her back. Maybe there was some divine reason that Jaanvi had found Sharan's phone when he was in the shower last night, had wondered who the call was from, had been bold enough to redial it. Maybe it was time the truth was out, and all three of them could be freed from the lies they were living.

'You aren't happy with her,' Mary said. 'Now that this has happened and she knows something, let's put everyone out of their misery.' She stepped around Sharan's black-topped desk, crouched down to his seat, wrapped her arms around his stiff legs. She closed her eyes and rubbed his thighs, just the way he liked, began working her skilled fingers upwards, letting the momentary quiet that had settled between them burnish into the intimacy they had shared just two nights ago, as they cruised a star-stroked sky.

Sharan pushed Mary's hands off him, like they were filth. The force of his movements stunned her. She fell over backwards. Sharan made no attempt to help her up, swivelling his chair around instead, so the back of it was to her, to stare out the window.

'You're crazy,' he said. 'This is over. Get out.'

Mary stood up, trembling.

'GET OUT!' he screamed, still facing the window.

She left his room, went back to her desk, picked up her bag and left.

Xavier Fernandez opened the door and saw his swollen-eyed friend, the beautiful and sexy girl next door, standing in front of him, drenched in the downpour. The rain landed on the balcony outside his flat, found a tiny gutter and the drops cascaded obediently down it.

He stood back to let her in. She sat down at a small corner table, its surface cluttered with old newspapers and dusty dishes. Xavier came towards her with a towel, a spread of peonies across the threadbare fabric. She stood up, allowed her friend to wrap it around her, felt it chafe against her skin. Her lips quivered, with cold, and shock. Her clothes clung to her. She reached for the plastic pearl buttons on her blouse, one at a time, and slowly undid them, sliding her arms through the sleeves, holding the towel against her breasts. She stepped out of her shoes, so the top of her head was now at Xavier's chin. He couldn't believe what was happening, but stayed quiet, not wanting to puncture the intimacy that he felt bloom between them. For years, he had dreamed of this. And now, here Mary was, wet and warm, so close he could feel her breath on his chest.

He raised a hand towards her cheek, and for a second she flinched, but when he rested his palm there, she leaned into the enfolding warmth of it. She lowered her wet head onto his chest. Now, his finger was on her bra strap, his other arm around her waist. Down in the compound, she heard the neighbourhood children laughing as they stomped through muddy puddles, not thinking of the slaps they would get later for coming home so dirty. Their gleeful shouts were the last thing Mary heard as she let Xavier take her by the hand and lead her into the bedroom.

# TWENTY-NINE

Bharat wanted to see me, said it was important. He suggested we meet at Ghetto, which I'd never been a fan of – too dark, not adequately stylish – but he talked me into it, saying he needed a change from the Aer/Amadeus vibe, a place he could wear shorts to, chill with a Kingfisher, listen to The Doors, maybe shoot some pool while he waited for me.

I sidled next to him, kissed him, let his fingers play with mine beneath the table. He had ordered plates of stuffed mushrooms and skinned potatoes. He put his arm around my shoulders and pulled me into him, our bodies touching intimately. I let him. I had no qualms about running into anyone I knew here.

'There's something you should know,' he said. 'I could lose my job for telling you this. Client confidentiality. Do you know a guy called Ravi Dutta?'

'I know of him.'

'He and your cousin, Karan, were in my office the other day, meeting with the CEO. Only the really big deals get heard by my boss. He asked me to sit in. They are raising capital to win a major petroleum pipeline contract between Kenya and Uganda. Ravi has already come in with a significant majority. They are looking to my firm to provide the rest.'

'Oh,' I said.

'The way it's structured, if they win the bid – and I know Dutta, whoever he has to pay off, he will – they will take it to Badshah. And if Karan gets the company, Dutta will be installed as CEO.'

'That's a lot of ifs,' I said. 'But, why?'

'That part's not clear. But everyone knows Dutta's reputation. He likes carving up companies. If he gets Badshah, you can say goodbye to it.'

❦

Milan and Pawan were in the study in their home, sitting at opposite ends of a leather-covered table, both on their laptops, a mass of papers laid out between them.

Rajan threw himself onto a couch at the farthest end of the room. My mother had asked me to pick him up from school, take him for his dentist appointment and look after him for the afternoon, so I had brought him with me to see our cousins. I wanted to share with them what I had heard about Karan and Ravi.

My cousins looked not in the least bothered about it.

'Don't you think it's a serious thing?' I asked them, exasperated.

'Please, Soh, why must you turn everything into a drama?' Milan said, barely looking up from his screen. Pawan switched tunes on the iPod, propped it up on its speaker dock and filled the room with jazzy, mellow music.

'We need to allow for the possibility that some outsider is vying for the family business and then it will go to none of us,' I insisted. 'Why aren't you worried?'

'Because it will never happen,' Milan said. 'It can only happen if Baba thinks Karan's proposal so magnificent that he hands over the keys to the empire to him. But if the old man had any inkling that the son of Chandru Dutta will one day be sitting in his chair, he will kick Karan out so fast, the fool won't know what hit him.'

'But how will he know what Karan has in mind?' I asked. 'Bharat told me about it, but nobody else is supposed to know. Client confidentiality.'

Milan looked up at me now, a naughty smile lurking at the edges of his lips.

'Then we do what we Bombayites are so damn good at,' he said. 'We start a rumour.'

I asked Milan and Pawan to show me what they were working on and they complied eagerly. They had put together an impressive PowerPoint presentation that began with the basics – Badshah was India's third largest steel producer in the private sector, the country ranked fourth in the world's output, the industry had taken a beating as a result of the recession, but had started to recover.

'The business has really been running itself,' Pawan said. 'It has been the source from which all else has come. For Baba, the steel business remains his pride and joy. His sons could never match his passion for it.'

'So we asked ourselves a simple question,' Milan continued. 'What is the best way forward? How do we make steel sexy?'

Anytime I had thought about that particular component of the Badshah business, a mass of confusion would descend around my head. I would overhear snatches of conversation between Baba, my father and my uncles – stuff about coking coal and ingot and pig iron – and my eyes would glaze over. The plants were noisy and hot and, to my mind, filled with danger and sweaty men in hard hats. Steel might have been Baba's first love, but to my mind, there was nothing remotely enchanting about it.

'What about a dragon?' Rajan suddenly piped up. He had been so quiet all this time, I had forgotten he was there.

Milan and Pawan continued to talk, ignoring their young cousin.

'I'm reading a book with an evil dragon,' my little brother persisted. 'You can make one of steel, it could fly, like rockets do, with jet fire. You'll have to make it really light so it will stay in the air. It'll be cool!'

Pawan looked up at Rajan, then at me, then at Milan, before leafing through a stack of papers in a folder at his side. A bright smile lit up his face. He stood up, walked to where Rajan was lounging, held my brother's face between his hands and kissed him on the top of his head.

# THIRTY

Jaanvi was alone at home, her legs curled up beneath her on the couch, working on a needlepoint image of a bucolic meadow, the stitching tight and neat. Her eyes, behind small wire-rimmed glasses, were puffy, exhausted. She told me she had suspected Sharan's infidelity for a while – the phone call the other day had confirmed it.

'He tried to lie,' she said, sounding defeated. 'He told me it was in my head, there was nothing going on, it was some big misunderstanding. No matter what, he can never be honest.'

There were no tears as she told me this. She was all cried out. 'I asked him to move to one of the guest rooms,' she said. 'He goes there at night, after everyone is asleep, makes the bed in the morning before leaving for work. You know how it is in this family; appearances are important.' She smiled weakly, toying distractedly with the frayed edges of her needlepoint canvas.

'Do you want him back?' I asked.

She shook her head. 'I'm done,' she said, softly, definitively.

We were both quiet for a moment, considering the implications of what she had decided. Marriages that had crashed and burned were increasingly common among Bombay's elite – too much money, access to recreational drugs, nightly drinking binges, spouses who had long ago stopped relating to one another, these were all common stories. I don't know why I had thought my family to be immune to it all. I envied the conservatively old-monied, the staunch families of Delhi and Calcutta who, despite coffers that were bursting at the seams, eschewed alcohol and meat-eating and ostentatious displays of wealth, whose men married simple, good women. It was possible to be loaded and live a quiet life. Understatement had been Baba's credo, from the earliest days of his ascent but it had become something that those who had come after him – his grandsons especially – defied.

'I can't imagine this family without you,' I said. 'It will feel lonely to me.'

Now, a tear rolled down her cheek, dripped onto a yellow sunflower she had just finished embroidering. 'To me, it has always felt lonely,' she said.

# THIRTY-ONE

*Today Asha, daughter-in-law number two, came to see me. Sohana had told her that Jaanvi had decided to leave Sharan*

*'She says he's a lying cheat,' Asha said.*

*'She cannot go,' I said.*

*There has never, in the history of the Badshah family, been a divorce. I wasn't only thinking of the reputation of the family, when I heard this news. Jaanvi is the daughter of our good friends. We took her with no dowry, even though they could have given everything. We knew she could be the girl who would settle that scoundrel of a grandson of ours. We promised her mother and father we would keep her safe and happy. We could not return her now, four years later, broken and miserable.*

*'How?' Asha said. 'Sohana tells me Jaanvi has made up her mind.'*

*'Wait. I will tell Baba,' I said. 'He will fix it.'*

*In the evening, I stood outside the dining room door. Baba and Sharan were inside and I had to press my ear to the door to hear what they were saying.*

*The cook came out of the kitchen, saw me like that and ran off. I turned the doorknob and went in. I had every right to be there; this was my family, my grandson. Baba had asked me to stay out of it. But I had had enough of sitting alone and saying nothing.*

*Baba was walking up and down. Sharan was sitting at his usual spot at the dining table, as if waiting for a Friday-night family dinner to begin.*

*'It's that Catholic girl, isn't it?' Baba said. 'Your office girl?'*

*'She's my secretary,' Sharan corrected Baba.*

*'I don't care if she's the goddamn Queen of England.' Baba said. 'You get rid of her.'*

*"The damage to my marriage is done,' Sharan said. 'At least Mary makes me happy.'*

*'Happy?' Baba said. 'Do you think I care if you are happy?'*

*'I know you do not,' said Sharan. 'You don't care for anything, except to control everyone.'*

*I had never heard anyone talk back to Baba before. I respected Sharan a little more for it. He was foolish to do so, but it made him less weak than I knew him to be.*

*'What did you say?' Baba growled.*

*'I'm leaving now,' Sharan said. 'I will make my own decisions about my life.' Baba stepped in front of him.*

*'I'm not finished,' Baba said, his face red with rage. 'Sit.'*

*'Sharu,' I said, appeasingly. That was my nickname for my oldest grandson. 'Please, don't go like this. Sit. Let us talk. Shall I call for nimbu pani for you?'*

*I knew he would listen to me. He sat down again. I took a seat opposite him, my back to my husband.*

*'Let me understand what is happening,' I said. 'You have fallen in love with another woman. This is correct?'*

*Sharan nodded.*

*'And you believe it is fine for Jaanvi to go home to Africa and this girl to become the new bahu of the Badshah family?'*

*'I didn't say that,' Sharan said. 'I don't want to be treated like a child. I want to make my own decisions.'*

*'What do you want, then?' I asked my grandson. Baba kept quiet.*

*Sharan looked like he had not slept for many days. He also looked scared. I wanted to hug him, like I did when he was small, when he had a fever or fell and scratched his knees, playing with the other boys.*

*'I don't know what I want to do, Dadi,' he said. 'I am sorry I have made a mess of everything. But I am not happy in my marriage. Jaanvi is a good woman. But we are not a good fit.'*

*'I am sick of listening to this nonsense!' Baba shouted. 'Sharan, all this talk of happiness is*

*meaningless. We cannot allow for your marriage to end. Get rid of the girl. Patch things up with Jaanvi. There is nothing more to be discussed.'*

*Sharan stood up again. This time, I knew he would not sit down.*

*'Fine,' he said. 'I will do as you say.'*

*Baba's shoulders slumped, relief crossing his face.*

*'On one condition,' Sharan said. 'You give me the company.'*

*That night, dinner was sealed in glass containers and put away in the fridge. Baba only wanted tomato soup and a toast with two slices of cheese. I sat next to my husband. I wanted to touch his hand, perhaps even stroke it. But something happens to old married couples; they stop touching each other.*

*'That boy can go to hell,' Baba said. 'He dares try to blackmail me.'*

*Baba had forgotten that at one time, he was going to give everything to Sharan anyway. He was the most hard-working of all the boys. That was before Baba started to play this stupid game and make his business the prize in a competition.*

*But my grandson still had no right to demand. I knew Baba would never forgive him.*

# THIRTY-TWO

It was a glorious Sunday morning and Bharat and I were reclining on striped towels, draped over chaise longues by the rooftop pool of the Oberoi. An American woman in a tartan bikini played with a five-year-old in the shallow end, stopping intermittently to check on his arm floats.

'Hope the bloody kid doesn't pee in the pool,' Bharat said, opening one eye and looking over.

'What do you care? Doesn't look like you're getting in anyway.'

He sat up, tossed a tube of sun tan lotion over to me.

'Here,' he said. 'Do me.'

I got up off my seat, perched on the edge of his, and unscrewed the cap on the tube. I squeezed the pink, fragrant lotion onto my hands and began massaging his chest slowly, letting my fingers get coiled up in the curlicues of hair.

'Nice of your client to let you have his room for the weekend,' I said, moving my fingers slowly down his lean, muscular shoulders and arms.

'Yeah, he was going off to Ahmedabad for a couple of days. Couldn't be bothered to check out and check back in again, so he told me to enjoy the facilities on his dime,' he said.

'Some people just have money to burn,' I smiled. I had to admit, it was bliss to be out of Bharat's depressing apartment, to be able to be alone with him somewhere else.

'Do you realize, this pool is shaped like a pair of testicles,' he said.

I turned around to look and let out a laugh. When he was sufficiently slathered, I went back to my chair, but left my arm draped over the side, letting his fingers toy with mine. It was quiet up there with just the soft murmur of people talking on the other side of the pool. It would get busy later. But by then, Bharat and I would be back in the room, enjoying the privacy, the luxury, the slight illicitness of it all. I smiled in anticipation.

'Dude! What are you doing here?' A loud voice shattered the peace.

Bharat suddenly dropped my hand. I took off my sunglasses. We both sat up.

'Hey, Manoj, how's it going?' Bharat said. He stood up. His back was sweaty. His bathing suit dipped down at the waist, revealing an elastic imprint.

'I heard you were living in Mumbai now,' the man said. He was considerably older than Bharat, overweight, a short, clipped mustache atop his thin lips. 'Are you staying here?'

'Just for a couple of days,' said Bharat. 'I have a serviced flat in Worli.'

'I'm in from Jeddah for a week,' he said. 'Lunch?'

'Yes, of course,' Bharat said, reaching for his phone.

Manoj glanced over at me, raised his eyebrows. 'Who is this then?' he asked of Bharat, as if I were deaf and mute and unable to speak for myself. I stood up, adjusted my cover-up, wiped my sweating hands on my front.

'Oh, this,' said Bharat, stepping aside slightly, to make room for me. 'This is Sohana. Just a friend.'

I turned to look sharply at Bharat, while still remembering to smile courteously at Manoj. I wasn't quite sure what I was to him, but 'just a friend' certainly wasn't on my list. Bharat looked at me hesitatingly, like he knew he had done something he shouldn't have.

The two men exchanged numbers, shook hands and mustachioed Manoj waddled off. The way I glared at Bharat, I was surprised he didn't run away after him.

'What?' he said, easing himself back into his chair.

'What do you mean "what"?' I said, still standing. '"Just a friend"? Really? What you and I do together, tell me, do you do that with all your friends?'

'Come on, Sohana,' he said, pulling me down next to him. 'Don't be like that. The guy means nothing to me. 'Friend' covers everything. Why should I tell him what you are to me?'

'Okay,' I said. 'Fair enough. But if you're not going to tell him, at least tell me. What am I to you?'

He smiled nonchalantly, picked up a magazine and proceeded to flick through it, ignoring me. 'Chill,' he said.

I stared out at the ocean, which today looked a surprisingly sparkling shade of blue, like it did in all the travel brochures, but almost never in reality.

'I have a better idea,' I said, gathering my things, astonished at the anger I felt roiling inside me. 'YOU chill. I am going home.'

'Sohana,' he said, exasperated, putting the magazine down so it flapped against his lap. 'Come on! It's a beautiful day. We have a suite to ourselves. Stop being so pathetic.'

I realized, in that moment, that I must have reminded him of Tania, or at least what I believed her to have been to him, based on what he had told me – I was whining, demanding, a little bitchy even. Bharat needed a 'chill' sort of girl, someone to spend languid afternoons with in hotel rooms, someone to meet for lunch and tea and drinks and dinner and yet someone who would not fully absorb him into her life, not really, not ever.

But I didn't care if he thought of Tania at this moment, as he stared at me, the two of us at a stand-off. Right now, I even felt sorry for her. I held my clothes in a small pile against my chest, fumbled to find my left flip-flop that was hiding under the chair. Without saying another word to him, I walked away.

The next afternoon, my mother came into my room, waving an invitation card. Her friends, Sarita and Harish Sawney, were throwing a twenty-fifth wedding anniversary party in Abu

Dhabi. She had mentioned it to me weeks ago, but after everything that had happened, we had let the occasion pass us by.

'Sarita called this morning,' my mother said. 'She's upset that nobody from our side is going.'

Much of Bombay society had already left, carting new duds from Anjalee & Arjun Kapoor and baubles, freshly chiseled by Bapalal, that would somehow have to be secreted back into India. The Sawneys had flown in a party planner from Paris to craft five different events taking place between Dubai and Abu Dhabi, one of them involving camels. I had no trouble believing the rumour that they had told their event guy to 'go beyond lavish'. Like swimming-pools-filled-with-Dom Perignon lavish. Like airport-tarmac-sprinkled-with-emeralds lavish. Not literally, but that was Harish Sawney's sensibility. If there was one thing he was good at, it was finding the most adventurous ways to spend money.

'Maybe we should go, just for the last night?' my mother asked. I looked at the invitation, which I was sure cost more than Rajan's schoolbooks for the year. They had impressively hired Barry Manilow to perform at the main black-tie shindig at the new St Regis Hotel in Abu Dhabi.

'You think, Ma?' I asked.

She shrugged. 'Just for a change,' she said. 'Also, it's a top-class crowd. You might meet someone.'

Her words prickled. I had a few missed calls from Bharat since our fight the previous day. I hadn't been in the mood to speak to him. I knew he thought I was overreacting, and perhaps he was right – why couldn't I just 'chill', be cool, let things unfold?

So, even though I might have wanted to tell my mother, 'actually, Ma, I have met someone', how could I? At my age, every prospect was a serious one, a likely suitor. At my age, I wasn't messing around anymore. A mere mention of Bharat would bring on a cavalcade of questions, family members would be rounded up, his background and personal history investigated, decisions made on both our behalf. I couldn't do that to him, especially if I was, indeed, a 'friend' he happened to have an exceptionally good time with.

Maybe it would be okay for me to be open to whatever might lie ahead. Two days in Abu Dhabi, away from the drama created by my adulterous cousin and his impending divorce, away from my own feelings of failure, away from the stresses the family was under, sounded exactly like what I needed right now. Just my mother and I, dressing up, air-kissing, guzzling champagne (well, at least I would), and wallowing in the shallowness of a society event that was all flash and dash, but where not a single soul would be stirred. Not that I was going there to get swept off my feet, necessarily. I was going there to get swept up in the superficiality of the moment, knowing that afterwards, all that would be talked about would be the number of lobsters boiled, the cases of whiskey consumed, the imported tulips, the Burmese rubies and who had flown in by private jet. There would be not a word about a gentle whisper between husband and wife, a loving look exchanged, a tender caress, because none of these things would happen; this couple would be too busy celebrating their twenty-five years of togetherness to have a genuine moment of it.

In the ballroom of the St Regis, it took us a while to find the host and hostess. We had to merge with the silk-and-chiffon-clad throngs, the air around us a sneeze-inducing melange of Guerlain and Dior. My mother and I were bumped along in the general direction of the

Sawneys, who were encircled by a triple layer of well-wishers. Sarita squealed when she saw my mother and grabbed her tightly. Her husband stood next to her, a behemoth of a man, more in girth than height. It wasn't just his wealth that had quadrupled since I had last seen him.

'Hi, Uncle,' I said. 'Congratulations. This is amazing.' It was. Even in the overindulged landscape of my life, this was an extraordinary fete, the walls draped in chartreuse silk, amber-coloured chandeliers suspended from the ceiling, the soft tinkle at every turn of pure crystal champagne flutes being delicately clinked together. A string quartet, not including a young man with tousled blonde curls strumming on a gold-flecked harp played near the far end, barely audible to the chattering crowd. Barry Manilow was being saved for the postprandial entertainment.

The circular tables were festooned with tiny bronze birdcages and jade-hued square candles. Each place was piled with anniversary souvenirs – blue Tiffany boxes and cashmere wraps embellished with bugle beads, goodies a hundred times more valuable than the wedding presents the couple would have received two and half decades ago.

'Harish, it's really beautiful,' my mother said. He beamed, red-faced, already drunk, not even midway through the cocktail hour. I smiled to myself, imagining him inebriated by the end of this long night, lying under the table, trying not to throw up.

Now, he smiled genially at my mother and me, his teeth stained brown from too many cigarettes, a pinch of fat caught in the lushly-embroidered neck of his Nehru jacket. He hugged me again, this time lingering just a bit longer than I felt appropriate, rubbing his hand up and down my back. He had a reputation. His wealth bought him many things, including a married mistress in London – the wife of one of his employees. He had reportedly given her a three million pound pied-à-terre in Kensington.

Their twin daughters hovered nearby, two massive nineteen-year-olds draped in identical lehengas of russet red, so large-boned that I was reminded of a Swiss ski chalet. This, after all, was a showcase for them as well, their parents silently telling one and all, 'see what we have, what we can give you, if you would just take one of these girls off our hands.'

Sarita stood next to her husband, that pretty, dazed look on her face perfected by socialites of note. Her foundation was two shades too light, her hair big and puffy and lacquered into place, giving her the look of a confused kabuki dancer.

Dangling from her ears were the most obscenely extravagant earrings I had ever seen. They were the size of an outstretched palm, fine filigree platinum overlaid with glistening layers of diamonds that dragged her lobes down so that just looking at the weight of them made me cringe. The rumour was that Harish had called his guy at Graff Diamonds and instructed him to create an anniversary present for his wife that would be worth a million dollars for every year they had spent together. These earrings were from a full suite, although Sarita had wisely chosen just to wear part of it now. The earrings were captivating, the star of the party, one of the reasons so many were converging around the couple. They were like their own tourist attraction. Harish pushed up against me and I got an unavoidable whiff of him, of sweat, seediness, desperation, despite all he had. If Sarita could put up with that for a quarter of a century, she had earned every carat of those diamonds.

Midway through dinner, I had to escape. I had run out of smiles and small talk. There were no worthwhile single men to speak of. The champagne buzz had worn off. My shoes pinched my toes. I excused myself and returned to my room, upstairs. As I rummaged in my purse for the key, I heard a giggle down the end of the corridor and looked up to see one of my mother's friends from Peru, who we had just spoken to downstairs, being gently pulled into the suite of a man who I knew not to be her husband. I shrugged; nothing seemed to surprise me anymore.

Back in my room, I checked my phone after I found a less torturous pair of stilettos. Bharat had texted again. It might have been the champagne, or because a few days had passed since our argument, but I texted him back; I figured he'd suffered long enough. 'Out of town. Will call when back.'

Feeling a little lighter, I freshened up, rinsed my mouth with Listerine, put my happy face back on. I made my way back to the elevator. It glided downwards smoothly, and then stopped on the fourteenth floor. The doors opened.

'Going down?' I heard a man's voice call out, unseen. The doors started to shut again. A button was pressed; they re-opened.

In stepped Martin Veitch.

# THIRTY-THREE

I gaped. So did he. I leaned against the wall of the lift.

'Shit,' I said, for lack of anything more expressive.

'Sohana,' he said.

'Oh my God. I can't believe it. What the hell are you doing here?' Seeing his face took me right back to that night, the night he left me to be humiliated at Dome. In a second, I remembered what it felt like when Raghu showed me how I had been swindled. I remembered the shame that had blanketed me for weeks afterwards. It was because of this man that I would never fully resurrect myself in the eyes of my family and I hated him.

'I can't believe what you did to me,' I said, not waiting for him to reply.

'It's not what you think,' he said. 'You gotta hear me out.'

We arrived at the lobby. I stayed in the lift.

'Let's get out here,' he said.

'I'm not going anywhere with you,' I said.

'Please, just to talk. I beg you. Please.'

We stepped out. There was a lounge in the middle of the lobby where, earlier today, my mother and I had enjoyed a demitasse of Turkish coffee, scented with rose water and cardamom and sampled plump, sweet dates. Martin led me to a small table. 'So this is how you're spending my twelve million dollars? Hanging out at luxury hotels?' I asked Martin bitterly.

'No,' he said quietly. 'Look, I know you hate me. You have every reason to. But your money is safe.'

'Really?' I said, loudly. 'If that is so, why did you just disappear? What the hell are you playing at?' My voice rose with every word; I was furious.

Martin looked at me earnestly. I realized now how out of place he looked here, in a T-shirt with shorn-off sleeves, tattoos down one arm, chinos and yellow sneakers. He was carrying a small plastic bag, printed with the name of a local supermarket. I could see through it. Inside was a bottle of water and a half-eaten sandwich.

'I hate myself for what I did,' he said. 'But you have to believe me, I didn't touch a penny of that money. It's in an account, where it is protected. Either I use it for what it was intended, or I give it back to you.'

'What are you talking about? The deal is off. You didn't get the rest of the funding you needed. I signed the contract. I forfeited. You fooled me.' I had a dull ache on the side of my head. I called for some ice water.

'I got the funding,' Martin said. 'My lawyer told me to put that clause in there for my own protection. I was never intending to use it.'

I stared at him blankly.

'But I was instructed to wait, to not proceed with the deal until further notice.'

'What are you talking about? I asked. 'Instructed? By whom?'

Martin was quiet for what felt like an age. 'Your brother,' he said.

'What?' I said. 'What does Armaan have to do with any of this?'

A long pause again. He didn't look at me. 'He contacted me three days before the announcement. He told me not to go through with it.'

'What? Why?' I exclaimed.

Martin took a deep breath. 'When I was nineteen, I got into trouble. Accessory to armed robbery. Someone got shot. I spent four years in jail. Your brother found out about it. He tracked me down. He told me that if I showed up that night and we launched our deal, he would tell everyone you were doing business with a convicted felon.'

'Wait ... what ... I don't understand...'

I felt faint. My brother? Going behind my back like that? 'I don't believe you,' I said, defensively. 'My brother would never do that to me.'

Martin reached into his back pocket and pulled out his BlackBerry. He scrolled down and turned his phone around to show me. I grabbed it. There it was, a list of exchanges between Armaan and him. I stopped reading after the first few.

'But, why?' I asked.

Martin put his phone back into his pocket. 'He said you weren't ready and he was trying to protect you. I knew it was bullshit though. I know about your grandpa, what he's asked all you guys to do. Your brother didn't want you to get there first.'

People from the party were leaving now, a bejewelled mass filtering out through the glass doors into waiting cars. My mother would be wondering what had happened to me.

'I wanted to call you.' he said. 'But what was I going to tell you? That your brother was a shitbag and I a coward? I felt so ashamed of how things went down. But I didn't know what else to do. I was finally doing something worthwhile with my life. I didn't want it out in the press that I was a felon. I thought I'd wait a while, let things cool down. I guess I preferred to be written off as a cheat rather than have you know the truth about me. I had some meetings in Dubai, the week before I was supposed to come to see you, so I just hung out here. I've got some deals going on in Abu Dhabi and Oman. I'm here at the hotel to meet someone. Can't believe I ran into you. I haven't touched a dime of your money. Look, I even eat cheap.' He held up the plastic bag, desperate to diffuse the tension.

I leaned over, put my head in my hands. What he was telling me was crazy. I would never ever, in a million years, have expected Armaan to behave like that, to stab me in my back. But there was no disputing it; I had seen the texts. And, thinking back, maybe it did make sense. Armaan had never really encouraged me in any of this, had seemed incredulous that I even wanted to give it a shot. I thought of how he had conveniently come home from his trip to Warsaw just hours after my Dome event, how he had acted all shocked and offended that I had even tried to get this business off the ground.

How he had gloated at what had happened to me and had made me feel so bad about it that I'd almost apologized to him. And through it all, he had known the truth. The anger I had felt towards Martin had found a new home. Right now, I hated my brother.

'I know it's too soon for you to make any decisions,' Martin said. 'But we're both here. You know the truth now. I still want to make this happen, but it's your call.'

'I can't think about that now,' I said, picking up my purse. 'I need to get out of here. I'll call you after I've had some time to think.'

I ran back into the ballroom, looking for my mother.

# THIRTY-FOUR

'I'm sorry, but I still don't believe it,' my mother said. 'It makes no sense to me. He is your brother.'

We were on the tarmac at the airport, on our way home. Plans to stay one more day in Abu Dhabi, perhaps drive into Dubai, had been quickly shelved. Sarita had wanted to host a luncheon for my mother, but when I told my mother about Martin and that I wanted to fly back home to confront Armaan, she agreed. At that point, neither of us were in the mood for fancy society lunches.

'Martin showed me the texts. He wasn't making it up.'

My mother stared out of the airplane window for a while. In the sun, her grey roots looked steely against the rest of her darkly-dyed hair.

'I can't believe what goes on in this family,' I said, tearfully.

'Maybe Armaan has a point,' my mother said.

'What?' I asked, aghast.

'Why should you be doing business with a criminal? He just wanted to protect you.'

'If that was the case, Ma, why wouldn't he just have told me? Instead, he snuck around my back, communicating with a guy that I was in business with, and then humiliated me in front of the entire family. When everything fell apart, he saw how miserable I was. Even then he didn't have the guts to tell me the truth. He pretended he didn't know anything, that it was all my fault. Why would any brother put his sister through that?'

My mother had no answer, because there wasn't one. What Armaan had done was horribly wrong, but my mother was too fiercely devoted to her son to say so. She had always wanted to believe the best about him. She had never taken sides in any of our fights and was not going to start now.

'We will be home soon,' she said. 'We will get some answers.'

The only sound that could be heard was that of gunfire, loud and violent, coming from Rajan's room, where he was playing video games with a friend. They had been sequestered in there with sandwiches, wafers and Coke, instructed by my father not to come out until the grown-ups were done talking. They seemed only too thrilled to comply.

Armaan sat on the edge of the couch, as if ready to bolt at a second's notice. His face was ashy, half-moons of sweat had started to form beneath his armpits and seep through his shirt.

'Is it true?' my father asked.

He nodded.

'Why?' I yelled out. 'I don't get it. You knew how much it all meant to me.'

'Of course I did,' he said. 'It was a damn good idea you had. You were the first among all of us to come up with something.'

'Then, why?' my father asked.

'I had been talking about it with Ekta and…' he began.

'She was behind this?' my mother said.

'It was her idea to hire a private investigator in the States who could find out about this guy, Martin. When we got the information, we used it to protect Sohana. We only wanted to make sure she would be okay.'

'So Ekta is behind it,' my mother said again. There was a quiver in her voice. It was one thing to believe the worst about Armaan. But the worst about his girlfriend ... my mother had no problem with that. Now she was angry.

'If you wanted the best for Sohana, you would have talked to her about it when you found out about Martin,' my mother said. 'You did not. You kept it to yourself, from all of us. You let her plan an expensive party, at which you were conveniently absent. You let her stand there, alone. You let her fail. Don't you dare say you wanted to make sure she would be okay.'

'Ekta felt it would be the best way,' Armaan said.

'Your Ekta seems to have lots of clever ideas,' interjected my father. 'I think I would like to hear them for myself. Go, now, pick her up and bring her here. I want to talk to her.'

Rajan finally came out of his bedroom after his friend was summoned to his own home. He sat in the dining room by himself, eating a dosa. I went in to join him, ruffled his hair and kissed his forehead. He playfully pushed me away, wiping the kiss off with the back of his hand.

'What's all the drama, Didi?' he asked.

'Just stuff,' I said. 'Nothing for you to worry about.'

'I saw Ba on his way out,' he said. 'He looked like he was crying. I've never seen him cry before.'

'First time for everything,' I said.

The key turned in the lock. Armaan and Ekta were back.

She walked in, pristine and glossy, like she spent every Sunday afternoon lounging around at home in Michael Kors jeans and an Alexander Wang top. She was decked out in black and white, with the exception of the ruby bangles my mother had given her the first time we had met her, her official welcome-to-the-family gift. In all the times I'd seen her since then, she had never worn them. But there they were on her bony little wrists, obvious reminders to us all that they had been gifted to her with love and affection by the parents of the man she had every intention of marrying.

Now she had a hesitant, even fearful, expression in her eyes, but her big white smile was determined to counter that. There were stiff hugs, cool kisses, hot cups of tea. Everyone settled down on the couch, like politicians about to negotiate a detente, instead of a well-meaning family relaxing together on a weekend afternoon.

'Ekta, there is a problem,' my father said, ever the master of understatement.

'Yes, Uncle, Armaan told me everything on the way here. Please, let me explain.' She was practised and self-assured, I'd give her that.

'Armaan had informed me of Sohana's plans,' she said. 'I was very proud of her. What a smart girl, I thought.'

I wanted to slap her smug face. 'But I know she is inexperienced in such things. I have a friend in America whose brother is a private investigator. I asked him to look into Sohana's potential business partner. We had to make sure he was an honest man.'

'If that is so,' my father asked, 'why did neither of you tell us what you were doing? And when you discovered Martin's past, why did you threaten him with it and make him fearful of coming here? That is blackmail.'

My brother and his girlfriend looked at one another, each waiting for the other to answer.

'We didn't want to hurt Sohana's feelings,' Ekta said weakly, speaking of me as if I wasn't there. 'We felt that the less she knew, the better. Easier for her to think of her business partner as a conman as opposed to someone who once drove the getaway car after a burglary.'

'Oh, so better to wait until I've made a total fool of myself, is it?' I asked, furious. I stood up now, staring down at the awful woman in front of me. 'Ekta, I have tried to like you. Really, I have. But you are a fake. All you can do is tell stories. You didn't want me to succeed, so you found a way to sabotage what I was doing. You need Armaan to win, because all you care about is our money! You're a psychotic bitch!'

Now Ekta was on her feet, towering over me. She looked as if she were about to slap me. Rajan, hearing the shouting from the next room, came running in, his eyes wide open. By now, everyone was standing. My father told me to sit down and shut up.

'Ekta, you played with me too,' he said. 'You allowed me to think my daughter was a fool, that she had lost my money.'

'Oh, please, Uncle,' she said. 'The whole town knows that twelve million dollars is nothing to you.'

My father's face darkened. 'Why is it, Ekta, that it's always the people who come from nothing who have the least respect for everyone else's money?' my father asked.

Ekta's smile vanished.

My mother shook her head and sighed deeply. For a moment, the living room turned silent, everyone's rage privately simmering. My mother stood up, went into her bedroom and reappeared with a blue velvet box. Ekta's eyes lit up at the sight of my mother approaching, bearing another gift. Relief crossed her face. This was all going to be over; she would be forgiven.

My mother pressed the small knob on the box that released the spring mechanism, causing the top to pop open. It was empty. She held out her palm towards Ekta.

'Please return the bangles you are wearing,' she said. 'This wedding will never happen.'

# THIRTY-FIVE

In the morning, a vast bouquet of flowers was delivered to the house. In a flat, golden box alongside it, lay a pale rectangular piece of fabric. I unfurled it to see that it was a small, white flag. The card attached to it read, 'Truce?' It was signed, simply, 'B'.

I stepped into my room and called him.

'Crap. What a story,' Bharat said. He had had a craving for the cheese fondue at Moshe's, and we were sitting here now, both of us dunking chunks of bread into a yellow pool of cholesterol. My jeans pinched at my waist.

'Just thought you might want to know that Tania, though still a mean and conniving bitch, isn't the only one to blame,' I said.

'She still wanted to hurt you,' Bharat agreed. 'It's not relevant that your brother and his crazy-ass girlfriend got there first. At least now you know the truth, you can get past it.'

'Not quite,' I said. I told him that, after the showdown at my house the other day,

Armaan left to take Ekta home and had not yet returned.

'My relationship with my brother is kaput,' I said.

'He's in love,' Bharat said. 'That makes guys do whacked-out things. Trust me, I know.'

'I'm sorry I got so mad that day by the pool,' I said. 'I guess it was kind of the last straw.'

'It's okay,' he said. 'I've been thinking about it too. I should have handled it better.'

'So ... can I ask you something?' I said.

'Are we doing this now?' he asked. 'Like, having the conversation?'

'I think we have to,' I said. 'Don't you?'

He didn't answer. I forged on. 'What is this?' I asked, waggling my index finger in the air between us.

'It's fondue,' he said.

'Stop. You know what I mean. What is THIS?' Now, I gesticulated more pronouncedly, pointing to him, then back to me. 'What are we? What are we doing?'

He wiped his mouth with a paper napkin and leaned back in his chair. 'I really like you,' he said. 'I like being with you. You make me laugh. You're very sweet.'

'But?' I said.

'That's it. I'm not thinking past that. I like where we're at.'

He picked up his slender metal fork and pierced another piece of bread with it. I thought back to something that had happened with Nitya a few years earlier; she had pined after a man, Sunil, for a long time until finally, a mutual friend had stepped in and asked Sunil if he harboured any romantic feelings towards Nitya. When the friend called an anxious Nitya afterwards, to update her, he recounted Sunil's response as – 'He didn't say no.'

Nitya had thought that was good enough, until I'd told her otherwise. 'He didn't say no' was not an adequate reason to continue loving someone.

Right now, in this moment, Bharat didn't love me enough. I wasn't sure if he ever would. But I wasn't sure, either, if I wanted to hang around and find out. For now, though, I decided to let the matter rest.

'Let me ask you something else,' I said. Bharat looked up at me almost warily, like he didn't want to have this conversation anymore.'About the Vecco. Martin left the ball in my court. I can still move ahead, if I want. Should I?'

Bharat looked relieved at the change of topic. He wiped his mouth, leaning back in his chair.

'Honestly, Sohana, I don't know. I can't advise you,' he said.

'What do you mean you can't advise me?' I asked incredulously. 'We MET because you were supposed to be advising me!'

'Yeah, well, and see how great that turned out,' he said.

'Look, I know it was your brother and his chick that made the mess with the deal,' he continued, after a pause. 'But that doesn't change the fact that I still expected you to take the word of my lunatic ex-girlfriend. So let's just say that I don't exactly trust myself when it comes to you.'

He stared at me squarely and I stared back, both of us acutely aware that it was perhaps the most real thing he had ever said to me.

He didn't trust himself with me. He didn't really love me. He didn't envision a future for us. He didn't want to help me, or at least he didn't believe he could. I closed my eyes and rubbed my forehead, as if I had a headache, although I didn't. Behind my closed lids, I saw Bharat and myself, standing at the end of a road; there was nowhere else to go.

Nitya called and was her happy, gossipy self.

'So, the chit-chat everywhere is that Karan is planning something evil with that fool, Ravi Dutta,' Nitya said. True to his word, Milan had started a rumour.

'It's the talk of the town,' she continued, delighted. 'Even those air-headed wives, who don't know a stock offering from a gel manicure, are gossiping about it.'

Everyone knew that Ravi's father, Chandru, had long envied Baba's prominence. He too was wealthy, and respected – but he had always admired what Baba had done with his company, the way he had kept it family-controlled, resisted offers to sell or merge and thwarted the expected move to go public. Baba was obsessed with control; he wanted to answer to nobody – no board of directors, no shareholders. Not even his own sons. He was like an emperor, ruling with absolute power. And for all of Chandru's success, he couldn't quite match the legend that was Baba.

Ravi knew this and also knew he had to resurrect himself. He had almost destroyed his father's business. He had been sidelined in favour of a stepson. Now he wanted to bring Badshah to his father.

But taking my cues from Milan and Pawan, I was no longer perturbed by any of it. Because Baba still fully controlled Badshah Industries, his company was something he could gift to anyone, as he saw fit. If Nitya had already gotten wind of the rumours, there was no doubt that Baba had, too. Ravi's plans would go no further. Karan and Ravi had about as much chance of winning Badshah as the cobbler who worked around the corner.

'Full drama,' Nitya said emphatically, thrilled. 'But I'll tell you what nobody understands. Why Karan is doing it. What has he to gain by letting this other guy take over Badshah?'

'No clue,' I said, truthfully. 'But if I know my family, there will be some juicy reason.'

'In the meantime,' said Nitya. 'What are you going to do? Now that you can have the deal if you want?'

'I haven't figured it out yet, Nits,' I said. 'I feel like I need to talk to somebody about it, somebody I really trust, who can tell me what to do.'

I heard Nitya breathe deeply into the phone. 'For heaven's sake Soh,' she said. 'Stop looking to other people to give you the answers. You have everything you need. Go with your gut. It will never steer you wrong.'

❦

Mary hadn't yet had the courage to tell Xavier the truth. That she didn't love him. That she didn't want to be with him. That she had used him that one rainy afternoon, when she needed solace, and somehow it had become quite convenient to use him over and over again. He was sleeping contentedly now while Mary lay still next to him.

Since Xavier's parents had gone to visit relatives, she had been spending a lot of time in his flat. More than she really wanted to. In truth, she had nowhere else to go. Since the day of her fight in the office with Sharan, ten days ago, she had not gone back. She had called Mrs Behramjee, the company's human resources manager, had told her that a family emergency would prevent her from returning to work. In lieu of notice, she had forfeited the rest of her month's salary. The company was very strict about these things, said Mrs. Behramjee, sounding stern and officious, complaining loudly about having to find a replacement right away.

Mary couldn't bring herself to tell her parents that she was now without a job. Mary's father earned a little as a tutor, helping fifth standard kids learn useless things like the highest two-digit prime number. Mary's mother worked six afternoons a week at the neighbourhood beauty parlour, washing the hair of ladies with double chins, putting away the trays of dried up nail varnish, breathing in the foul odours of perm solutions.

Mary remained her family's main source of income – especially on those days (nights, mostly), when Sharan would give her a hefty cash bonus. On those nights, there was extra mithai on the table after dinner, a gas bill paid early for once, a reprieve for her mother from cutting the toenails of women with fungal infections.

So there was no way Mary could tell her parents that she was now, unfortunately, just another liability. Sure, she could find another job before long. But she had ruined her chances of getting a good reference letter from her boss. What would he say to recommend her? 'Her shorthand skills are excellent, her agility in bed more so. Shame my wife found out.' Mostly, she felt incapacitated by the thought of finding something else. She didn't want to send in applications and go on interviews, putting on a brave face and a happy smile and promising to do her best. She was in no mood to start all over again.

So since the fight at Sharan's office, she got dressed every morning, packed her purse with its regular contents – comb, lipstick, a packet of scented tissues, a book for supposedly reading on the train and a small sandwich for lunch – left her parent's home, and went next door to Xavier. There she would get undressed again, and climb into Xavier's bed. Sometimes he was there; as a freelance film editor, he made his own hours. When he was, they played, kissed, cooked together, watched TV. He didn't ask questions about her dismissal, and said he would help her to keep the truth from her parents, in order to protect them from unnecessary anxiety, for as long as necessary. He would happily be her alibi. For him, in many ways, Mary's sudden unemployment and her vulnerability, were a dream come true. He had long been in love with the girl next door. She had been unattainable for him, a vision in tight skirt and high heels who went to her big-city job every day. She was the girl he could never have. And here she was, in his bed, day after day, needing him. Perhaps all those Novenas he recited for his mother provided some bonus blessings.

But both Xavier and Mary silently recognized that this situation could not carry on forever. Mr and Mrs Fernandez would eventually return. Xavier's home could no longer be her hideout. Her limited savings would start to run out. She would have to start considering her options soon.

She could, of course, go back to Sharan, beg for a second chance. But it galled her no end that since the day he had turned his back on her in his office, he had made no effort to reach out to her. Anything could have happened to her – perhaps she had been so distraught that she had jumped in front of an oncoming train at the Dadar railway station. Or so agitated over her fight with him, that she hadn't noticed the gang of bad men sneaking up behind her on the street, who might then have dragged her off into a dark alley somewhere.

Sharan had not given any of this the slightest consideration. Clearly, she thought bitterly, he didn't care if she was dead or alive. Her fury at that fact had given rise to all sorts of other possibilities. She could try a bit of extortion, threaten to reveal their tryst to the world. But to what end? What did she want from him, ultimately? Money? Her job? His love again, even if she had never really had it?

No. Mary had to think carefully before she proceeded next. She needed a plan. It was precisely her lack of foresight that had led her to this moment, lying in a two-roomed flat in Mahim, its walls covered with garish pictures of Jesus and Mother Mary, shelves lined with cheap ceramic trinkets, a plastic shower curtain in the bathroom coated in mildew, a cluster of shoes at the doorway that tripped her up every time she walked in. This was not the life she had envisioned for herself. She needed to find a way out of it.

Xavier opened his eyes and glanced over at Mary. He kissed her shoulder and placed his hand on her thigh. She stirred. She wasn't really in the mood. She kissed him in return , gathered the sheets around her and slid out of bed.

Xavier watched her slip into a dress, run a comb through her tousled hair. These past ten days had convinced him that Mary was the right girl for him. His parents were returning at the perfect time. As soon as they were back, he would seek their blessings. And then he would ask this girl-next-door to marry him.

# THIRTY-SIX

*I went to see Gurdas today. My driver helped me up walk up three floors to the flat. How many lakhs we have paid him over the years, and still he has not moved from this dirty building in a lane in Santacruz.*

*Gurdas was sitting at a small white table, his fat legs stretched out, hair sticking out of his nostrils. He smelled of Vicks. He was seventy-five at least, but he looked much younger than that; not a line on his face. He only believed in Ayurveda.*

*Now he stood to greet me, folding his hands together. 'Sit,' he said. 'Tell me.'*

*He keeps the astrological charts of everyone in my family in a red plastic file, marked 'Badshah – Top Important'.*

*'Things have become very bad,' I said. 'Too many problems in the family. A curse has landed on our house.'*

*'It is only karma,' Gurdas said. 'I can do prayers for you.'*

*'I do not need your prayers,' I said. A small fan whirred in the corner but it was still so hot in here. I*

*pulled out a handkerchief from my purse and waved it in front of my face.*

*'I need you to look at the charts, see what is happening.'*

*Gurdas took out a small pair of glasses.*

*'For two grandsons especially,' I ordered. 'And Baba, of course.'*

*Depression had crossed Baba's path, Gurdas told me, explaining which planet was in which house until I told him to stop with all that nonsense.*

*'He feels alone,' Gurdas said. 'He knows his actions have caused family separation. This has brought him sadness.'*

*Baba had shown me no signs of regret about his decision. He was only angry, all the time. But perhaps this was his way.*

*'Tell me about Sharan,' I said.*

*Gurdas found Sharan's chart. Gurdas had told me four years ago, that Sharan and Jaanvi would make a fine match and have good children. He had never seen what had happened, that Sharan would cheat.*

*'A shadow has fallen on his home life, on matters concerning the bedroom,' Gurdas said. 'A little roughness. His eyes have gone to another.'*

*'In the beginning, why did you not tell me this would happen?' I challenged Gurdas now. 'Did you not see an affaire?'*

*Gurdas took off his glasses, rubbing his eyes with the back of his hand. 'Ji, please understand. In all such matters, we have free will. Other people will always cross our path. In every marriage. But we make choices. We are not slaves to lust'*

*'And now? What is to become of him?' I asked.*

*Gurdas made some calculations, scribbled some notes, muttered ancient Vedic words under his breath. 'There is a good chance for recovery,' he said, as if discussing the loss of a necklace. 'They can become one again. But for that, your grandson must show his heart.'*

*'Okay,' I said. 'Now tell me about Armaan.'*

*'He has gone to a woman with a black heart,' Gurdas said, consulting the charts. 'She is not good, this one. But another girl is coming for him, much better, more peaceful. But it is for him to decide. I cannot say where he will go.'*

*This was not good news for me. There are many things Baba believes that I do not agree with. But I do agree when he insists that a daughter-in-law can make or break a family. Jaanvi, even though Sharan says she is not a good match for him, has been beneficial for us. She is thoughtful and pure. Even if Sharan does not love her, we do.*

*'Bas, thank you,' I said, stuffing my handkerchief back into my purse.*

*'Wait,' Gurdas said. 'What about the girl? It has been long since we consulted her chart.*

*'Why not?' I said, sitting back down. 'I have come all the way.'*

*Sohana's chart was at the back of the file, uncreased and clean, as if rarely looked at – no matrimonial prospects to investigate, no medical issues to gain advice on (with God's grace), no career or academic matters. It was as if there was nothing at all to her life.*

*'See,' he said, pointing to lines and squiggles and numbers I had no interest in.*

*'As of now, Mercury is in her seventh house. Strongly.'*

*'What does that mean?' I asked.*

*'That it is in her mind to own a business. The house is strong. So the business can be profitable. There have been some missteps, but they will be corrected. She can have a good future in business. In matters of matrimony, there is some delay.'*

*I did not care about the last part of what he said. I have stopped being concerned about Sohana's lack of marriage prospects. When I see the unhappiness of the others, I think, let her be happy, let her remain unmarried for now. Till thirty, even.*

*But what Gurdas said about what is in my granddaughter's mind, about owning a business, this made me very happy.*

*'What must she do?' I asked him.*

*'For marriage, nothing. Just wait.'*

*'No. Not marriage. For business.'*

*'She must show force,' he said, looking at the chart a second time. 'She must show determination. If she does not know these things as of yet, then she must learn them.'*

*The traffic was worse on the way back. My driver was doing his best to push his way through as fast as he could, but I said, please don't rush, there is no need. We will get home sooner or later. Nobody is waiting for me.*

*I had been glad to hand over an envelope to Gurdas stuffed with notes, which he held to his forehead with both palms and kissed before putting into his pocket. He deserved every rupee, for I felt better now than I did when I first went to see him. Maybe there was hope for Sharan, who would fix his marriage and finish things with that cheap woman who could never, ever become a Badshah. As for Armaan - he is a smart boy and if he is too blind to see his girlfriend for the fake person she is, then he deserves to be miserable.*

*I was most happy to hear of Sohana, about the change in her destiny. The missteps Gurdas spoke of, she has already made them. I have been told of*

*Armaan's betrayal … he and that girlfriend, daring to hurt a sister. What happened was not Sohana's fault. This wrong will right itself. She will have another chance and this time, she will be smarter. She will make the most of it.*

*I thought of Gurdas' great-uncle, Mithu Maharaj, who had served my parents in the same way that Gurdas now serves me. Mithu had been my father's most trusted advisor. It was because of Mithu that I came to be married to Baba, even though just weeks before, I had sat with his brother Ram on the stairs outside my father's house, whispering to him in the night, listening to his dreams of the business he would one day build, the thing he had invented that nobody else had. We were in love when it was not allowed. These romances did not affect the nobility; we lived far, far above all that middle-class emotional nonsense. Mithu told my father that Ram was weak and a dreamer, someone who would never fulfill any ambitions. But Darshan, the brother – this was a good boy; smart and disciplined and a worthy welcome to the family.*

*'This is a good match,' Mithu had said to my father.*

*My heart drowned.*

*'She will bring Darshan great luck, a Lakshmi in his house. Think nothing that this young man now has no means. In his future, he will own the world.'*

*I did not care. I did not want a man who would own the world. I wanted the man I wanted.*

*'Your daughter,' he said to my father. 'She is the key. Like the Ganga flows from Shiva's head, all of Darshan's riches will flow from your daughter's hand. His life, his destiny, will start and end with her.'*

*Mithu was right. My husband's fortunes swelled more and more each year. Ram married his second choice, who lived in my shadow all her years, although I know he tried hard to love her. Me, I tell everyone – find someone good to marry, someone with a kind heart, forget all the nonsense about looks and money and upbringing, for a truly good person will make your life. Baba believes, as my father did, that it is not necessary to marry for love. And this is the truth that I live with, every day.*

## THIRTY-SEVEN

'What?' I said, pulling off my headphones and slowing down the speed on the treadmill. Nitya, running alongside, had flung a newspaper at me, opened to a particular page.

'Are you showing me Bipasha Bapu's abs again, because I really don't want to see them,' I said to her.

'Check it out,' she said, smiling cheekily. She indicated Mumbai Masala, a new column in the newspaper – our city's answer to the National Enquirer, where everyday people were part-time paparazzi, tipsters and informants. The result – seedy stories like, 'See Deepika Without Make-Up!' or 'Which Starlet Has The Worst Cellulite?'

I turned to look at the page in front of me.

'Is Socialite Bedding Hot Cricket Star?' a headline trumpeted. Below was a grainy image of my aunt Malini and Vivek Abbas.

'Oh God,' I said.

Nitya had started sprinting again, pressing the button on her treadmill to give it an incline. I stayed level and slow.

'So it's finally out,' I said. 'This is the last thing my family needs right now. Another scandal.'

I read the story quickly; the two of them had been spotted together at an airline lounge where, according to the witness, they were nestled together in the corner, whiling away the hours after their flight to Delhi was delayed. The accompanying photo showed Vivek in a baseball cap and sunglasses, a futile attempt at a disguise. He and my aunt were photographed at the snack buffet, lingering over reheated spring rolls, Vivek's arm around my aunt's waist. It was a photo that showed familiarity, if not intimacy, but one could so often be mistaken for the other.

'I don't get it,' Nitya said, wiping sweat off her forehead after ending her workout. 'What can Abbas possibly see in your aunt? He doesn't need her money or her connections. He has everything. And she's like a thousand years old.'

'Maybe he likes her company,' I said. I couldn't believe I was defending whatever might be happening.

'Please,' objected Nitya. 'Have you talked to your aunt recently? I've had more interesting conversations with my shoe.'

I tossed the paper on the floor. It was 9 a.m. By the time I got back home, the news would be everywhere.

My mother was in Armaan's room with Chanoo. Empty boxes sat around their feet, piles of clothes on his bed.

'What's happening?'

'Your brother has called. He's sending someone to pick up his things. He is moving in with that woman.'

I could see that my mother had been crying. 'What?' I said. 'That's not possible.'

I had thought by now that my brother's senses would have returned to him, that he would have recognized Ekta's malice and come back home. I usually admired men who stood by their women – especially given that Jag had not stood by me. But I knew this woman and she did not deserve anyone's devotion.

'He has made his decision,' my mother said. 'He's a grown man. I cannot stop him.'

My brother and I had not spoken since he had left that Sunday with Ekta. I was still mad at him, even though my mother had tried to convince me that he had been manipulated by that woman, that he would never have acted that way on his own. I realized it was going to take a long time to heal the rift between us. I would be willing to at least try, but with Ekta in the picture, my brother would never be able to see straight.

Still, I needed to reach out to him. Whatever he had done, the day we confronted him, he looked genuinely chagrined. He knew on some level that he had betrayed me. We needed to find our way back to one another.

I left the room, grabbed my phone out of my bag and called my brother. He answered immediately.

'Ba,' I said anxiously.

'Hey, Soh,' he said. He sounded tired.

'I hate this,' I said, crying into the phone. 'You're my big brother. I hate what's happening.'

'I know, I messed up, Sis. I'm sorry. Really I am. Nobody meant to hurt you.'

I wanted to refute him, tell him that Ekta actually intended to do just that. But this was not the time for it. I needed to keep him on the phone.

'But don't move out,' I said. 'We can't fix things if you're not around.'

'They expect me to choose between them and the girl I love,' he said. 'I choose Ekta.'

'But please, Ba, after everything that happened, what she did ... we are your family ... I am your sister.' I slumped down on my bed. After all this, he still couldn't see it. Whatever Ekta was doing to my brother, she was exceedingly proficient at it. She had snared him and she wasn't about to let go.

'I'm not getting into this with you,' Armaan said, a new resolve in his voice. 'I'm sorry about what happened and it's your choice to accept the apology or not. You need to know, we've decided to elope. Have a private wedding somewhere. Maybe Athens. Ekta likes it there.'

'Greece?' I asked. The randomness of it all was staggering. Armaan had always said he wanted a Hindu temple wedding – small and simple, then the big blow-out party afterwards, here in Bombay, his home.

'She was thinking, on a yacht, off Mykonos,' he said. 'I really want you and Rajan to be there.'

'Ba, you're not making any sense!' I said. It was as if there was someone else inhabiting Armaan's body, cultivating thoughts for him that he would not ordinarily have possessed, impacting his life in the most bizarre ways. 'Firstly, you care nothing for Greece! Why would you want to get married there? And after everything that's happened, how awful your girlfriend has been to me, to this family, how can I come? Until she apologizes directly to me, I want to have nothing to do with her!'

There was silence. I waited a few seconds.

'Hello? Ba?' I said into the mouthpiece.

He had hung up.

My mother went to the temple after that, a slightly decrepit one in Churchgate that had become something of a satellite spot of worship for the extended Badshah clan. My mother liked the pandit there, Ketul Maharaj, who had an uncommonly pleasant touch. He had returned recently from several years in Long Island where he'd performed Hindu rituals for mixed marriages and knew just how to tailor his services for the younger, more attention-deficit, set. Unlike so many of his kind, who used mild fear and light intimidation to push their agenda, he never chastised when someone overlooked Shivratri or Ganesh Chaturthi. Instead, he laughed, pushed warm prasad into our hand and said, 'It's cool! Next time!'

I knew my mother had seen Ketul Maharaj, because she seemed in a better frame of mind when she came back; no longer tearful, quite resigned to the decision her firstborn had made. I had no idea what he had said to her, but I felt very grateful to him, just the same.

'Did you see this?' I asked her, showing her the Mumbai Masala item of that morning. She glanced at it, nodded and got on with what she was doing, rearranging her closet.

'Wait, Ma, don't you think it's weird? Aren't you curious about what's going on between Malini chachi and this cricket dude?'

'Don't say 'dude', Beta. It's not proper use of the English language.'

'Ma, come on!' I stressed. 'Look at the picture! They're all over each other.'

She pulled out a trove of sari petticoats, arrayed them in a rainbow formation on her bed and began colour-coordinating them. I suppose even the most pampered needed something to do with their days.

'Sohana,' she said, tugging at a stubborn string of one of the garments. 'You will learn, with time, that many things are rarely as they seem. And, beyond that, you really shouldn't believe all the trash you read. Now, tell me, is lilac lighter than lavender?'

# THIRTY-EIGHT

*We are already on the second Friday of the month, the days are flying by so fast. Dinner at home tonight, with everyone. Last night, Milan called up. He said, 'Dadi, me and Pawan have something to show Baba tomorrow, after the dinner. Is it okay?'*

*He did not have to ask my permission. We have all been waiting. Baba and I will not go on forever; death will come for one of us soon. I feel in my heart, that, neither Baba nor I can depart from this earth before we know who is stepping into my husband's shoes.*

*I am happy for one thing, that at least Jaanvi will come to dinner tonight. I phoned her, to see how she is, bechari. She sounded alright, quite fine. Or maybe that is how young women sound on the phone when they speak with their husband's grandmother. Maybe she could not let her voice break and allow me to see into her heart, because I am an old woman and she does not want to scare me. I should tell her, 'Jaanvi, it is okay, I have seen more pain than you know.' But that she will be here shows me that she still considers herself a part of this family, for now.*

*Karan, that boy should not show his face here, but he will, because he is desperate, like his brother. Baba heard about Ravi Dutta's plans – or I should say, Karan's plans for Ravi Dutta. Baba was shaking with anger when his friend called him to warn him. Karan does not yet know that we know. But Baba will find a way to tell him.*

*Armaan, he has left the family it seems, and gone away with that dumb girl who talks too much and is full of ego. I told Baba that he should still have a chance. He is still a Badshah, still a grandson. Baba had to agree with me and said, yes, if Armaan comes with something, then we must listen to him, give him a chance too. It is the right thing to do. But that will not happen for now; that boy is too busy washing his girlfriend's feet in rose water to be thinking of his own future.*

*So that leaves just Milan and Pawan, two brothers joining as one, which makes me happy because they have never done anything together. They are smart too, both of them, in different ways. They could be very good for the future of our family business. I did a special puja this morning, asking Krishna to please bless the boys with good ideas and a good show, so this may all be finished and we may go back to being a family again.*

*This morning, after the vegetable seller left, the lady in the house next door sent mishti doi for Baba; she knows how much he likes it. It was cold and creamy, sweetened with khajuri guda. When the boy who was delivering it was leaving, I had an idea. 'Ek minute,' I shouted to him. I went with him to speak to his memsahib, who is very jolly and kind and after half an hour, the boy came back, his face washed, hair oiled back, ready to work.*

*Our Friday dinners are mostly the same; we have tandoori chicken and naan and biryani, chana masala and paneer, always excellent, but not very special. Milan sometimes, when he sits down, jokes with the servants and asks for a menu, because it is the same food he gets at Copper Chimney or Khyber.*

*Once, after Sohana took those cooking classes, she made a full dinner for us all at home. It was nice. Something different. A salad with big soft balls of cheese, pasta with salmon, some Italian rice with spinach and mushrooms, a very good sponge cake with cream and fruit for dessert. Afterwards, Baba called it 'foreign food' – food he has to eat when he is staying at a fancy hotel when he travels. It is not what he wants to eat in his own house. He is not happy unless his fingers are covered in oil and there are mustard seeds in his teeth. He likes only the best of our home food, rich and heavy, and he can eat it every night.*

*But I wanted something special on the table today. So I asked the lady next door if I could borrow her cook, Tipu – an ordinary Bengali man who should be a famous hotel chef, so lovely is his food. Those hot afternoons when he comes over with a big dish of panta bhat, which most people hate but I love, with the crunchy fried onions on top or a plate of sandesh, laid out like small golden leaves, I am so happy, and I eat to my heart's content.*

*Tonight will be a special night.*

## THIRTY-NINE

I sat on the couch, next to Jaanvi.

Everyone was here. Even Armaan. He had the good sense to leave that witch of his at home. But at least he came and was talking civilly to our parents during appetizers.

'So, what's the deal?' I asked Jaanvi, indicating Sharan at the far end, in deep conversation with Prakash Chacha. She had lost weight, no doubt a function of the recent anxieties in her life. But there was something else, a lightness to her, like she was done shedding tears.

'I'm still here,' she said. 'He promised me it's over with that woman. He's been home a lot. We are talking.' She lowered her voice. 'A person comes over twice a week. A therapist. It is helping.'

'Wow,' I said. 'Can't imagine Sharan in counselling.'

'Yes, he resisted. But I made it a condition of my staying, at least for now. And, you know,' she said, 'it takes two people to wreck a marriage. I have a role, too.'

'Maybe,' I said, putting my hand on her lap. 'But he was the one out screwing someone else, so don't beat yourself up too much.'

Karan occupied a small couch next to his mother, both of them oddly quiet and removed from the rest of us. I stared at Malini chachi, who, compared to her usual overdone appearance, was, tonight, almost ascetic. She wasn't wearing those long, fake spidery eyelashes she loved, didn't roll in here with tons of bling weighing her down, in red or leopard print, everything shiny and skintight. Her hair, usually big and brown and teased, was pulled off her face, which was remarkably clear of eyeshadow and blush and gloss, like she had come here straight from having a facial. I was reminded of how striking she was, how easy it had been to forget the beauty behind the mask of make-up that was her shield. She looked apprehensive and distant. Everyone had read the article about Vivek Abbas and her and she knew they had construed what they believed to be the truth. Her husband, Amit Chacha, who arrived separately, did not greet her.

Pawan and Milan were already there and had disappeared straight into a study downstairs, where they were setting something up – a fact which created a sense of anticipation among us. I wanted dinner to be over, so we could get to their presentation.

There had been a lingering unease over us all these many months, us cousins coasting by on a finely cultivated image, an inherited reputation and wealth that was not created by our own hand. Something was shifting. As I had seen, all too painfully recently, a price must always be paid for privilege.

Since returning from Abu Dhabi, I had been thinking about Martin, about what to do next. The money was safe, still earmarked for what it was originally sent to him for. I knew the truth about my potential business partner. It was up to me to decide if I wanted to move ahead or not. Bharat and I had talked about it repeatedly, and he had made the sensible suggestion that if it had once seemed a good idea to me, and if nothing else had changed, then it was still a good idea. What Martin Veitch had or hadn't done when he was nineteen had no bearing on it. And Nitya, true to her word, would call me every so often with a business proposition; her latest was a start-up that would turn a TV into an interactive social network.

Still, I knew I wasn't ready to make any decisions yet. I was still digesting everything that had happened and wanted to keep my options open. Right now, I didn't want to think about it.

'I've been seeing someone,' I said to Jaanvi now, apropos of nothing.

'Excuse me?' she said, half-smiling.

'I don't know why I just told you that. Nobody knows. Not my parents, Nobody. Well, Nitya. That's it. I'm not sure if it's going to go anywhere.'

Jaanvi had laid bare her devastation to me over her husband's infidelity. There was a small part of me that felt I needed to reciprocate her trust.

'I really like him. He says he likes me, too. But that's all he says. He doesn't express very much.'

'Sometimes, a man doesn't have to,' Jaanvi said, a little wistfully. 'Sometimes, with a man, you just know. It's in how he touches you, in what he says when darkness comes, and it is you and him. You know, Sharan put a seven carat diamond on my finger, but it didn't really mean anything. Your man, will he fight for you? Will he still love you even when you are least deserving of it?'

These were not questions I could answer. I was grateful when the dinner gong rang.

# FORTY

The food was better than ever. Bengali cuisine, a first at the Friday dinner – Shukto with big chunks of bitter gourd, cholar dal and luchis, machher jhol – fire-red and spicy, chingri macher malaikari – big prawns in coconut paste. Everybody thanked Dadi, as if she had been in the kitchen herself, pulling the veins out of the prawns' heads. I made a mental note to ask Tipu from next door if he might teach me a thing or too.

We left the dinner table, our bellies full, happy with whisky-soda, vodka-tonic, red wine. In the hall, we called for tea and coffee. The twins were standing next to the TV, their computer was plugged into it, like executives at a conference, waiting for their employees' attention. Preeti Chachi and Prakash Chacha sat closest to them, my uncle nodding with encouragement, like a new father pushing a toddler to walk.

Everyone in the room became quiet. Pawan started to speak.

'Oh, please, wait,' interrupted Malini.

Everyone turned to stare at her.

'I am sorry, boys,' she said to Milan and Pawan. 'This will not take long. I hope you don't mind.'

Milan looked irritated, but said nothing. This was supposed to be his and his brother's big night. I could see him thinking – typical of bloody Malini, to come along and mess things up.

'I am sure everyone here read the newspaper the other day. With the photo of me ... and Mr Abbas.'

She wiped her sweaty right hand on her skirt. In her other hand, she held a folded hankie. Under the bright chandelier, she looked pale. Amit Chacha could not face her.

'I know how it looks,' she said, her voice trembling. 'I know people have been talking. I need to tell you, there is no truth in what they are saying. I am not that kind of a woman.'

'Then what is going on, Bhabi?' Preeti asked, in her kindest voice. 'We would like to know. I am sorry, please don't take it the wrong way.'

'I am very ashamed,' Malini said, as she started to cry. Her husband shifted in his chair, uncomfortable at his wife's display of distress.

'I have kept a secret. From all of you.' She was crying harder now, wiping her eyes on her hankie. 'I have been drinking, alone and a lot, for many, many years. Vivek … Mr Abbas … he is helping me. He has been through this himself, I am sure you know of it. I have gone to AA meetings, in Kurla, where I am sure to not meet anyone. I met him there. Between us, there is nothing. Just friendship. But I am no longer drinking.'

She looked down on the floor. In the room, nobody spoke. It was so quiet, I could hear Baba breathing through his nose and Malini stood there, as if awaiting her verdict in court. My mother went to her and led her back to her seat, fetched some tea, rubbed her back. I looked at the three brothers, all of them confused and unsure how to react, not knowing what to do with this new information.

Milan caught my eye, his brows raised. I don't know why, but I felt an uncontrollable urge to laugh. I popped a cube of sugar into my mouth, just to give it something else to do.

My aunt, Malini, could hold her liquor better than anyone I knew. She was also not the sort of woman to ever concede any sort of weakness, which alcoholism most certainly was. I had seen her with Vivek in person, had seen the way her fingers caressed the front of his shirt as she looked up at him. It was not how one looked at a mentor or a friend. Every time I had seen her, the woman had a drink in her hand. Except for tonight, when she stuck with soda water, almost in preparation for this. She deserved a Filmfare award. If Malini's story was true – that she was indeed an alcoholic in treatment with the biggest cricket star of the day – then I was Kate bloody Middleton.

A sudden stillness had flopped over the room, everyone's face bearing grim, tragic expressions. Malini wrung her hands earnestly, the words of her mea culpa hovering in the cool air. Rajan, who had had his earplugs in the entire time, was the first to speak up.

'Are there any more jamuns?' he asked.

At which point, I lost it. I let out a loud laugh, trying to cover my mouth. Everyone stared at me, horrified at my hysteria.

'Sorry,' I said, wiping away tears with the back of my hand. 'Sorry, sorry.' I bit my lip.

Baba stood up. 'I have heard enough,' he said. 'I am going upstairs. You,' he said to Milan and Pawan. 'You will have to wait till another time.'

The rest of us picked up our handbags and shawls and phones. Milan and Pawan's big night did not happen. Even in what was supposed to be Malini's darkest and most disgracing moment, she was able to spoil something for someone else. The woman had a gift for it.

# FORTY-ONE

Mary sat on the toilet, waiting for the two glasses of water, she had just drunk, to take effect. In her right hand, she held a small white stick, poised to use it as soon as her bladder sprung into action. For three days, she had felt queasy and light-headed. Today, after eating too much of Xavier's masoor tonak, she had thrown up in the parched plot behind the building. There was only one possible explanation.

She readjusted her position, closed her eyes, and slipped the stick between her thighs. When she pulled it out, she shook it slightly, as if using a thermometer. Then she peered at the little indicator window and waited.

After work that evening, Xavier went alone to a nearby bar, where he ordered a Kingfisher and a plate of masala papad. It had been a long day – they were still in the middle of post-production on an action film and he had spent hours deciding which of the car chases and raunchy nightclub songs should be cut. If it were up to him, he'd eliminate all of them.

But it was not up to Xavier. Few things were. He was his parent's sole son and since his three married sisters were scattered around India, it was only he who could live with his aging parents, take care of them, say the novenas for their long life.

As he wiped the condensation off the beer bottle with his fingers, Xavier thought of how he couldn't wait to step into the sort of life he imagined a film editor should have – a flat in Navi Mumbai, its walls covered with trendy poster art, his collection of brass ashtrays on a corner table, black leather couches and a modular kitchen. It would be here that he would entertain his friends with chilled wine and chaat, looking out over the seascape, enjoying a cigarette on the balcony. Xavier had had high hopes for his future. But as he had learnt, life rarely unfolds the way you imagine it in your head. Sometimes it is better, many times it is worse, but it is never, never exactly as you envision it.

In his case, at least until Mary showed up, his life had been a disappointment. He worked less than he wanted to, and most of his income was spent providing for his parents, what with doctors who would suggest one medicine or another to fill the holes in his mother's brain and various hearing aids for his father, each more useless than the last.

Since Mary's miraculous appearance on his rain-washed doorstep, he was galvanized into action. He had spent the next morning calling the studios and production companies and animation houses he had worked with, reminding them he was around and available, a move which had yielded some good results. He had opened the small rusty safe at the back of his mother's closet and pulled out the tiny plastic bag in which she kept her grandmother's wedding ring, the one she said she would give to her son to present to his intended. It was a squat diamond set in grimy gold, and he had put it in his pocket to take for polishing. He was going to be Mary's protector, her guardian, the great love of her life. When her job had been snatched from her, and she was so distraught, she had come to him, hadn't she? She didn't go to the man, whoever he was, that she had claimed to love. That other fellow could never love Mary the way Xavier did.

He pulled out the ring from his pocket now and gazed at it under a flickering overhead light. An old Air Supply tune played in the background.

He was earning more, he had a ring in hand, his love in his bed; he could not fail.

Things were finally turning around for him.

Mary slipped the key into the door of her parent's flat and called out as she entered, as was her habit. The place was tiny, her parents would hear her come in, even if they were at the furthest point in the flat. There was no need to announce herself.

'You've come,' her mother said, standing up from the couch, where she had been watching Balika Vadhu, her hand in a packet of chevda. 'Quick, Daddy will be home soon. Let's put dinner on the table.'

Mary followed her mother into the kitchen, warmed up the oil to start frying pooris. The pungent smell of the garlic pickle that filled a small stainless steel bowl made her want to retch. She turned her attention to the atta, rolling out the dough and throwing it into the hot oil, standing back as it started to pop.

'What are you doing?' Mary's mother shouted at her, pulling the ladle out of her hand. 'Turn it! It is starting to burn!'

Mary smiled distractedly at her mother, apologized. The last thing she could think about now was food or cooking. Ever since taking that pregnancy test in Xavier's bathroom earlier today, she had felt as if she was not even in her body. She was carrying a child. She had repeated the test, twice. A small being, the size of a grain of rice, was growing inside of her, right now.

Sitting there, on Xavier's toilet, she had started doing the math, based on her limited memory of school sex education, counting back the days to when her period should have started, when conception might possibly have happened. Numbers had never been Mary's strong suit. She had consulted her calendar, writing down the day she had walked out of Sharan's office and right into the enfolding arms of a new lover. She worked out the last time she had been with Sharan, after their helicopter ride, both of them giddy with champagne and the high that comes from being above the world for a while. Forty-eight hours later, she had fallen into Xavier's bed.

So here she was, weeks later, without a job, lying to her parents, pining over a married man, unable to decide whose baby she was carrying. Mrs Carrasco, her teacher in convent school, who wore nylon pantyhose that pressed down the coarse hair on her legs and whose large behind spilled out over the narrow wooden chair she occupied, would faint if she knew that one of her best and most pious students was now in the position of not knowing, for sure, who the father of the baby she was carrying was.

It didn't really matter though, Mary thought to herself, as she laid the fried pooris out on a paper napkin and let the oil seep out. It didn't matter at all.

# FORTY-TWO

Matunga Dada asked me to meet him in Shivaji Park. His friends would leave by 6.30 p. m. to head home to a dinner of dal and rice and raita, with grandchildren who ignored them. He wanted to stay a while longer, to find a spot on the low stone walls around the circumference of the park where, he and I would sit together and eat apple slices.

I had come from Bharat's flat. He had called earlier, inviting me over, and I went because I was already beginning to miss the way he touched me. We hadn't talked about the Vecco or anything of any import. He had opened a bottle of wine, and I sat next to him on the couch, giving in to the moment. It was all right, because I knew that after I left his place, nothing would change; he would be the same man he was at Moshe's, who had said I didn't mean enough to him and I would be the same woman who was sure that that wasn't enough for me. We would inhabit a moment filled with need and longing and that would be the beginning and the end.

Now, I got to the park early, and stood on the sidelines for a while, watching little boys, all in white, play cricket on the red-sanded field, thwacking bats that missed many balls. A part of me dreaded the future of this supposedly great sport in this great country, where eight-year-olds would rather familiarize themselves with the wii console than the wicket.

The gravelly earth was the colour of russet, and I twirled my feet around, making spiral patterns, leaving my bare toes covered with a fine layer of what looked like sun-burnt sindoor. The air had cooled and I fished my pashmina out of my bag and wrapped it around my shoulders. A schoolgirl rode past me on her bicycle, mottled purple streamers flying from a rusty bell. Her hair was slicked with coconut oil, fastened with a sparkly barrette and she pedaled in sandals, carefree as the summer wind.

I cast a glance around the park, looking for Dada. I saw him at the furthest end, his back to me. He was not alone. My Dadi was with him. I was taken aback at the sight of it. I had never seen them alone together and it was startling to watch them talk like friends and confidantes, as if they had spent their whole lives together, which, of course, they had. Only, looking at them, you wouldn't suspect that they'd spent their lives separately, not as one. They weren't even touching, but there was an intimacy there, a gentleness that I don't recall ever witnessing between Dadi and Baba. I could see her face, and it was relaxed and full of an odd light, her wrinkles diminished, her eyes bright. It was the face of a woman in love, I realized in a bewildering revelation.

I was rooted in the red sand, unsure of what to do, whether to approach them or stay where I was. I looked at my watch – only 6.20. Dada was a stickler for time, and if he wasn't expecting me till 6.30, then I was to respect that.

Dadi nodded, in the way she always did just before saying goodbye, preparing to leave. Dada put his hand over hers, a sweet farewell. She turned and left, the same sunset-shaded dust that covered my feet now tinging the hem of her sari. Her driver started his engine as she walked towards the car, and she turned around once for her brother-in-law as she lowered herself in and was driven off.

I started to walk towards my great-uncle.

My eye was drawn to the other side of the park, where a kerfuffle had broken out over two auto-rickshaws that had collided, both drivers emerging from their small black and yellow cabs to swear at one another and assess the damage.

In front of them, I saw a car – Baba's old Mercedes, the one he had continued to use even though he could afford a thousand brand new ones. Through the open window, I saw the side of his face, pensive and grey, staring out at his wife as she got into her own car. From his vantage point, he would have seen everything.

He pushed a button to roll up the window and his car glided off. Mystified, I made my way over to Dada.

❦

*I had told Baba I wanted to go to Mahalaxmi temple. Actually, I was going to meet Ram at Shivaji Park. But I could not tell my husband that. I was so happy to see Ram. His cheeks were pink from his walk and he had been sweating. I took out my hankie and wiped his forehead. I think he was uncomfortable with me touching him like that.*

*He asked me about Sohana, how she is, what she is doing. I told him what Armaan had done. He did not seem surprised; Ram has come to expect the worst of us. I told him about Malini, that she said was an alcoholic but was not cheating on her husband. I tell him things because he does not judge, not even Sharan for carrying on with that cheap girl or*

*Armaan for being crazy about a vain model or Karan for turning into a terrible thief or Malini. Some of these things he already knew; the news is in the air, in a small place like Bombay it will get out, he says secrets cannot be kept here.*

*I wanted to leave before Sohana arrived, so she would not see me with him. I have wanted to tell her, about Ram and me, because I know how much she loves him, and also how much she loves me. But I cannot; she is still a young girl, so full of hope for the future. The family she wants to have one day, she has based that on the family she has now. I cannot destroy that for her.*

*Ram and I talked a long while, reaching some silent understanding, like we always do. When we speak, it is cool and calm. He has never been mad at me, no matter the foolish choices I have made, and I have honoured him always.*

*He told me what he thought should happen next. I was in agreement. It was not until I was in the car that I realized I left my hankie with him. But it is okay. It is the least I can do; after all I too have taken from him.*

*Now, Baba has told me he is hungry and he wants cheese toast for a snack. After he washes his face and changes and eats, Baba says he wants to talk to me. That it is important.*

# FORTY-THREE

Dada wanted some hot, roasted corn, so I ordered two. We munched on the cobs, the charred niblets sticking in my teeth. Near us, a small man with a large belly, jogged on the spot, his personal trainer, puffed up on steroids, barking orders at him.

'At least the poor fellow is trying,' Dada said. 'But there is no point, for he will go home and his wife will stuff him with jalebis.'

'Do you miss her?' I asked, randomly.

'Who?' he asked.

'Dadi.'

His face turned white.

'Your wife,' I clarified. 'That Dadi.'

His body, stiff just seconds ago, relaxed now. 'Of course,' he said. 'When a man loses his wife, he is never the same. Why?'

'Just,' I said. 'We have never really talked of her.'

'No, you were just a baby when she passed away,' he said. 'A shock to all of us. That TB, it is a terrible thing. How she suffered in the end. She would have loved you.'

I took the remnants of his snack from his knobby fingers, and deposited them in the nearest rubbish bin, its surface a whirl of flies. It was getting dark now; the park was slowly emptying out with just a few dedicated walkers plodding along.

I held out my hand and Dada eased himself off the bench. Our arms were linked as we walked towards Rohit, who was standing outside my car, smoking a beedi.

'Was there a reason you wanted to meet me today Dada?' I asked him. For the past hour I had been wanting to tell him that I had seen him with my grandmother and that Baba had seen them too. But the words would not come out. It felt wrong to speak of it, as if in so doing I would puncture the bubble Dada and Dadi seemed to sporadically inhabit, drifting in and out of it as their lives would allow. It was not for me to ask questions. There is a holy, guarded truth at the core of every family. This one, I had no right to.

'I have been missing you,' he said, as we got into the car. 'You are in my heart all the time. Many things are changing and you will be affected by them. With all that will be happening around you, you must not forget who you are; a Badshah, our only daughter.'

A dark rain started to fall. Rohit turned on the windshield wipers and boosted the air-conditioning. The wipers made a squeaky squish against the glass, the immaculate rhythm of them oddly relaxing. Had I not met Dada tonight, he would have made his own way home from the park, standing under an angry sky by himself, waiting for an auto-rickshaw to deign to stop for him.

I hated that he was alone so much, with only a young, unreliable servant to care for him – someone who would leave the moment a better-paying job came along. I hated that he lived surrounded by disarrayed memories, musty and doleful, without anyone to reminisce with. Ours was a large family, homes and spare rooms galore, with all the comforts that should have been endowed to not just an elder, but our elder, a kindly widower who had been mysteriously cast aside decades ago, but who loved his family anyway.

Once, a while back, I had floated the idea of having Dada come live with us, but my father said I wasn't making any sense, that Dada preferred to be alone, everyone knew that. I said to my dad, 'how do you know, when you have never asked him?' but my father waved me away, like he so often does, and no mention was made of it again.

The grand ambition with which I had started the year felt so distant now. I did not know where to tread next and realized that nobody could tell me. I wanted to ask Dada, but the last thing he needed was more pressure on his frail shoulders.

A great love had left me, to be replaced by a man who didn't seem to know what he felt for me. My brother had betrayed me. My father and uncles seemed resigned to their fate, to living out the rest of their years golfing and waiting to have grandchildren of their own. There were less benign ways to approach the beginning of the end of their lives, I thought; I should be happy for such small mercies. As for me, perhaps I wasn't cut out for any of it, no matter what Dada, Dadi or Jag tried to tell me.

Maybe my bid for Badshah Industries, as much as I hated to admit it, was not based on anything real. I had been caught up in a story someone else had told me, one that wasn't my own. I had wanted to live out someone else's happy ending. That fate had shown me to be so categorically misguided, I saw now, was actually a blessing. Whoever had sabotaged me – Tania, Armaan, it didn't matter. I would never have been equipped to run the company, had I won. If I was the right sort of woman – strong, noble, a force to be reckoned with – Armaan would never have done what he had done. But he saw me as weak, a small child to be trifled with. If that was so, then I deserved what happened to me.

I turned to look at Dada. His eyes had grown heavy. I removed my pashmina from around my shoulders and covered his body with it. I let him sleep.

# FORTY-FOUR

This time, Baba said he could not wait until the next Friday night dinner. He called his sons – who called their wives, who called the children – and he summoned us all on a Wednesday evening to his offices.

Something was going to happen. Something big. Baba had never, in all his life, demanded that his entire kith and kin arrive at the headquarters, summarily, without explanation.

Before I went, I needed to speak to Jag. Before I went, I needed to be armed. Bharat had failed me, on more levels than I cared to admit.

Every time I thought of Jag, I felt a pinch in my heart at the way I had humiliated myself the last time I had spoken with him; accusing him of having a woman in his life, as if he was not completely within his rights to do so. I recalled how sick with relief I had felt when he said it was his sister visiting, how that was an indication of my love for him, in spite of my pathetic efforts to extinguish it.

I called him on his cellphone. He sounded surprised to hear from me. 'I'm at home,' he said quietly on the phone. 'Shall we FaceTime?'

A few seconds later, there he was on my screen, with his weekend stubble, his mug of coffee, his slightly mussed hair, jazz in the background, his face so kissable, I wanted to cry.

'How are you?' he asked, two fingers thoughtfully over his lips.

'Yeah, good,' I said. I looked into his dark eyes, earnest, alone, focused. 'Actually, not good.'

'What's going on?' he asked.

Damn him, I thought. I was quite the bitch the last time we had spoken. I was carrying on with the friend he had asked to help me out. And still, there he was, kind, concerned, full of good intentions. It disgusted me, how lovely he was.

But it wasn't okay. Jag gave and gave and gave. I couldn't just let him.

'First tell me how you are,' I said. 'You look well.' I was lying a little. He had greyish circles under his eyes, his face a mass of preoccupation.

'I've been back and forth to Jersey,' he said, indicating where his parents lived. 'My dad is sick.'

'Oh, Jag, I'm so sorry,' I said. 'What happened?'

'It's okay,' he said. 'Don't really want to talk about it right now. Tell me about you.'

'All kinds of crap going down,' I said, giving in to his request. I told him what had happened with Martin, the betrayal levied on me by my brother and Ekta. He listened impassively.

'Wow,' he said. 'That's a lot to deal with.'

'You're not wrong about that,' I said.

'What do you need from me?' he asked.

'Baba has called a meeting for the whole family, in a couple of days. Something is happening. I need to be equipped. I suppose I need to know if I should proceed with the deal with the Vecco or not,' I said. 'It's still pending. I can have it if I want it.'

'What does Bharat think?' he asked.

I wasn't sure if his tone was sarcastic or not. Jag, I had always felt, didn't have a cynical bone in his body – none of that passive-aggressiveness so routinely displayed by beautiful boys of his ilk.

'He's sitting this one out,' I said. 'Won't commit.'

'Hmm,' said Jag, a shadow of a smile playing on his lips.

'So I'm coming to you,' I said. 'Do I do it? Do I not? Everything is in place, more or less. I could still have it, if I wanted.'

'Do you trust him?' Jag asked. 'Martin Veitch. Now that you know the truth about him, do you still trust him?'

'Actually, yes, I do,' I said. 'I think he's a good guy. I think he could have handled the whole thing better, but I understand why he did what he did.'

'Let me ask you something else,' Jag intoned, peering into the screen. 'The reasons why you wanted to do this from the beginning, to win the company, do they still stand?'

I hated him for asking the sort of questions that made me think, that forced me to be honest with myself. Why had I launched this bid, anyway? Why had I, Sohana Badshah, Bombay's most fabulous young socialite/heiress, wanted to do something as icky as fight over a company?

I had wanted to do it for him, for Jag. My uncle had cheated his father; I had wanted to right the wrongs. I had wanted to win Jag back.

'Partly, maybe,' I said. 'Firstly, I wanted to be taken seriously by my family. And then, well, everything that had come before. I wanted to fix that.'

I knew that he knew what I was talking about. Neither one of us needed to say it outright.

'And if there wasn't this challenge?' he asked. 'If your grandfather hadn't one day decreed that the company would go to one of the boys, hadn't just insisted that you all come up with a grand plan? Would you have done this anyway? Water cars? Is this in your future?'

I closed my eyes, lowered my head, fiddled with a hangnail on my pinkie.

'I think you have your answer,' Jag said.

# FORTY-FIVE

We were all sitting on the top floor of the Badshah Industries building, encircled around a glossy mahogany conference table. There was only water to drink. This would not be a long meeting.

Everyone was here. Even Rajan, who looked bemused as to why Baba would push back the time of the meeting until he was out of school. He sat now at the furthest end of the table, spinning around in a leather chair, braking with his feet.

Baba was the last one to walk in and assumed his rightful place at the head of the conference table, its seat taller and wider than all the others. A quiet fell on the room. Behind him stood Mrs Bose, the company's lawyer, an elegant woman in a blue pantsuit and small pearls in her ears. Dadi sat next to him, her hands clasped in front of her. Whatever suspense the rest of us were in, she was not, that much was plain.

'It has been one year,' he said, his voice a couple of octaves lower than usual. 'One year since I told you of my intentions. You have had one year to make your own plans. To show me something. To prove your worth.'

The room was so quiet, it as was if it were hermetically sealed, as if even air couldn't make its way in or out. At this point in the decline of Baba's mood, somebody or another should twitch nervously, fidget in their seat, come up with a flim-flam rationalization. But not now. Not today. Everybody could divine, to a person, that Baba wasn't in the mood to hear any of it.

'I have been sitting, all these months, waiting. I have been hearing things. Gas pipeline projects. New technologies. Defence contracts. Good things. Interesting things. I have been waiting. Waiting for you to come to me, one by one, and tell me.'

His dark eyes, shielded under shaggy grey brows, cast his eyes over us. 'But what have you done?' he growled. 'I will tell you what. Absolutely bloody nothing.'

Dadi rubbed her forehead with her third finger. Malini stared over at Amit, looking terrorized, as if someone had just stormed into her home, brandishing an AK-47.

'Sharan,' he said. 'You have been distracted by the wrong things. You are not the man I thought you to be.

'Karan, you are a fool if you think that I will let you give the company away to your friend, Ravi Dutta.' Karan turned white.

'Armaan, you have hurt your own sister. To me that is an act worth six lifetimes of bad karma. And Milan and Pawan, you…' The boys looked up, hopefully. They had done something, at least. They had prepared. They had tried.

'After you all left that night,' continued Baba, glancing sideways at Malini, 'I found a paper you left behind, from the presentation you did not get to make. Lightweight steel? Rubbish! Lightweight steel has been tried and it has failed. What makes you think you can succeed?' he snorted.

'Baba, actually, if you let us explain…' began Milan.

'No!' said Baba, thumping his fist down on the table so hard that a glass decanter of water at its center spilled droplets. 'I told you! Something bold! New! Exciting! Steel is not that! Steel is my home! I have lived there for fifty years and don't you dare think you can come in and show me a new room! You are young boys, out in the world, hearing things, knowing what is new! And you come to me with something old? You cannot imagine my disappointment in you!'

The colour washed out of Milan's face. He looked close to tears.

Baba rubbed his thick hand over his mouth, for a second shut his eyes. 'Tomorrow, I may be gone,' he said. 'I do not wish to leave without knowing that my company, my fifty years of work, will be looked after.'

'Baba, may I speak?' I asked, raising my hand tremulously.

'No,' said Baba. 'You may not. This is not bloody Parliament. I am not interested in hearing any opinions.'

Dadi reached out her hand, put it on Baba's sleeve to appease him. 'It's okay Beti,' she said, looking at me. 'Say.'

I stood up. I thought I would quiver, be full of nerves. But I was not. 'Maybe none of us are ready yet, Baba,' I said. I was thinking back to my most recent conversation with Jag. As far as I could tell, nobody had a clear vision, including myself. 'You have seen that. We have made mistakes. Maybe, for now, let our dads be in charge. There is no urgency.'

'There is,' Baba said darkly. 'For reasons I cannot share with you, there is an urgency. A successor must be chosen. Here. Now. Today.'

Now, finally, a breath broke out in the room. Cousins looked at one another, brothers and sisters-in-law were mystified, everyone bound by an all-encompassing confusion.

'Everyone. Stand up,' said Baba. Chairs scraped back. Everyone stood. Except me. Baba walked around the table, like a colonel inspecting a regiment. Mrs Bose followed. He walked past each cousin, in succession, staring at them cursorily and moving on.

He came to me. 'Stand up, Sohana,' he said, angrily.

'I'm not doing this, Baba,' I replied. 'This is all wrong. The whole thing is. The timing. Everything.You need to stop.'

His eyes, stern and gloomy, fastened on mine. He put his hand on my arm, and yanked me up. 'Sohana,' he said. I was now level to him, staring into the dark, angry eyes, shielded by their bushy brows. 'You tried. You brought us something. You failed. But only because your brother wanted you to. But it was a good idea. A water car. I like it. Carry on.'

He looked at my father and uncles, seated together. 'Sohana is my choice,' he said. He turned to Mrs Bose. 'Begin her training.'

The room was quiet no longer, its inhabitants erupting in a cavalcade of words.

'Wait,' I said to Baba, as he walked away from me. I was in shock. 'What? Wait!'

He continued walking. Everyone in the room was still talking.

My father rushed to my side, grabbed my hand, his fingers pressed into my wrist so hard, it hurt. 'Wonderful, Beti!' he said, in his eyes a mix of madness and desperation. 'This is good. Very good. From here, all things are possible.'

'We will hold a press conference day after tomorrow,' my grandfather intoned, as he turned to leave the room. 'You will begin preparing with Mrs Bose first thing tomorrow morning.'

'Wait!' I cried. 'Wait!' But nobody heard. I looked around. I had never been in this conference room before. It struck me, with alarming clarity, that a person who had never sat around a conference table should not be CEO.

There were things about this company I would never know. And there were things I didn't know enough about. Like what we owned. And where. And what I should do with them. If Baba had chosen me because of some idea I had about a water car, he was severely misguided, because I wasn't sure if I wanted any of that anymore.

This whole thing was ludicrous; I had no right being here. Everyone stared at me, their eyes saying the same thing. Milan looked at me, despairing, like I had taken away everything. Sharan had already walked out. Karan was talking in a corner with his mother. Armaan had his head in his hands. Only Rajan still spun in his chair, unconcerned.

My father pulled me aside. 'Fantastic!' he said, hugging me again. 'Now, with you at the top, I can still be here. Anybody you want can still be here.' There was a desperation in his voice and my heart cracked in two; he didn't want me to be his savior, he wanted me to be his puppet.

Across the room, Dadi stared at me and at nobody else. In her eyes, I saw the truth. That I was Baba's default; the only choice he thought he had.

Mrs Bose wanted to take me away. She said there was work to do. I shook her hand off me and went up to Milan.

'Listen, Milan, I had no idea,' I said. 'I don't understand it. I don't want it. I'm not ready for it. Baba is making a huge mistake.'

'Sure,' he said. He pushed his seat back, got up and walked away.

Almost everyone was gone now. Mrs Bose was conferring with Raghu outside the room. Only my parents remained seated at the table, helping themselves to water, whispering to one another.

I leaned against the large plate-glass window, staring out at my city, at the sea, grey and grimy, its white-tipped waves like frothy curlicues. If I craned my neck, I could see my special spot.

I should be happy. I was home. I was on top of the world. I had been chosen. As of tomorrow, I, Sohana Badshah, 27, would be at the helm of the biggest privately-held company in India. Overnight, I would be worth billions.

Only I wasn't worth anything – not the magnitude of my grandfather's trust, not the position of repository of my father's last hope. I wasn't worth the spot I was standing in. I wasn't even officially in yet.

But already, I needed to find a way out.

## COMING SOON

## The last book in the *Bombay Girl* series

The wind hit the back of my head, lashing my loose hair against my face, getting the strands entangled in my mouth. A spray of salty water misted over my eyes, forcing them momentarily shut. Across me sat a young, German couple, holding hands. They looked like they were on their honeymoon. I didn't think to ask them, I didn't care for conversation.

I was on a speed boat in the middle of the Indian Ocean, en route to the island of Lankanfushi, in the North Malé Atoll in the Maldives. In ten minutes, I would disembark, check into my villa in the resort of Gili Lankanfushi, shut the door and not talk to or see anyone for four days. If my parents called, I wouldn't answer. Even if Bharat called, I wouldn't respond. I had never before felt such an urgency for solitude.

Less than twenty-four hours ago, my grandfather had decided to hand over his billion-dollar company to me. Me! Unprepared, unqualified, ill-equipped me. I had thought for months that I had wanted it, had convinced myself that I was the best person for the job. Until I was given it. At which point, my resolve crumbled into a morass of self-doubt. I realized that I could not have been less deserving.

After Baba had made his decree, all my relatives – most of whom were no longer speaking to me – left the conference room, some in tears, others in shock, feeling profoundly the rejection that comes from being discarded, of being considered irrelevant by a grandparent. Baba did not couch his words tactfully. In fact, he lambasted them all individually for their incompetence. He had waited a year for one of his grandchildren to bring him an innovation that would startle him. For one reason or another, that had not happened. As a result, perhaps because I had at the very least made the biggest effort, he had chosen me.

Mrs Bose, the company's lawyer, had attempted to whisk me away, to have me sign papers and be lectured, instructed and prepped. There was to be a press conference announcing Baba's decision. I had no doubt, given my family's profile, fortune and standing, that the news would go viral. No matter how it was framed, I would still look like an idiot. So the previous afternoon, I did what everybody else had done. I fled.

'Where are you going?' my mother had asked, as I was pulling out clothes that Chanoo, my maid, would neatly pack later. I was still on the phone with my travel agent.

'The Maldives.'

'But ... but ... you can't...' my mother stammered. 'With everything happening here, how can you just go away?'

I ignored her. I had no reason to be mad at my mother. But right now, I was mad at everyone.

'And you're going alone? I cannot allow that.'

I stopped what I was doing for a second and turned to face her. 'Really, Ma?' I said, sarcasm lacing my tone. 'You think it's fine for me to become CEO of one of the biggest companies in India, yet I can't take a three hour flight by myself? Seriously?'

'At least ask Nitya to go along,' she persisted. 'Or maybe Daddy and I can take you...?'

'Ma! Please!' I shouted. 'I need to be alone!'

'But the announcement, Beta. Baba says he is telling all the media in two days! How can you...'

'The media can go to hell,' I said. 'And Baba can go screw himself.'

Now, it was my mother's turn to get mad. She snatched from my hands a top I had just pulled off a hanger and tossed it onto the bed.

'This was YOUR idea!' my mother said. 'You said you wanted the company! You begged your dad to give you money for your car project! Your daddy and I supported you the whole time. Here! Look! Now you've got it! Baba has said you are the best, that he wants you to run his beloved Badshah Industries! And you're miserable and flying to the Maldives? What is wrong with you?'

My mother was right. I suddenly remembered a line I had read from Oscar Wilde, years ago – 'In this world there are only two tragedies. One is not getting what one wants, and the other is getting it.'

Obviously, my mother was not going to sit down and discuss philosophy with me. She turned and left. I stayed in my room until the next morning, when it was time to leave for my flight. Nobody was around to say goodbye.

❦

I had friends who had vacationed at Gili Lankanfushi, who had raved about it. I hadn't taken much of it seriously. As I knew, from my own experience, rich people who had access to the best destinations in the world would rave of course; what was not to like about five-star this and luxury that and personal butlers and private-chef-prepared meals? If you had money, every trip was a dream, every sheet super-soft, every service impeccable, every outing the best you've ever had, until the next.

But this here, where I was now, was something else. It seemed almost wasted on the solitary sabbatical, such as it was, that I was on. This place was made for love and joy and intimacy and celebration – not the sad introspective state I was now in.

I stepped off the boat onto the jetty and was ardently greeted by my 'Ms Friday', a curly-haired woman with a beaming smile, who let me know that she could do anything I needed – book spa appointments and excursions and restaurant reservations and would be available to me twenty-four hours a day.

'Yes. But can you sort out my life?' I asked her, only half-joking.

While Ms Friday unpacked my few paltry belongings – I wasn't going to need much for my four days here – I told her that I did not want to be disturbed, that I would have all my meals in my room, that I would accept no phone calls unless I knew who was on the other end. She looked at me askance, clearly wondering if I was on the run from the law, if any moment now Interpol would be descending on this resort built on stilts, in the clearest azure waters of the Indian Ocean, disturbing its finely-cultivated sense of isolation.

I asked for a Mediterranean platter for dinner before she left. I picked out a soft pear from the wicker fruit basket and bit into it, letting its juice dribble down my chin. I flopped down onto the wide, pristine-white bed, with the mosquito net rolled up around it and gazed outside the wide, glass doors at the sublime waters beyond, that lay like a shimmering oceanic glaze, placid and calm. I didn't do what I always did when I arrived somewhere new – check my phone maniacally, log into Facebook, read my Twitter feed. I didn't want to know what anybody else was doing and I didn't want them to know what I was doing either. The irony was not lost on me; I had found what I thought I was looking for. But for now, I didn't want anyone to find me.

After dinner, which I washed down with a small glass of chilled Chablis, I retreated to the patio outside my room. It was dusk already. I spritzed myself with insect repellant and reclined on the large, elastic hammock, swaying under a crescent moon. There was not a sound to be heard. I so wanted some of the calm around me to seep into my soul. If I needed a place where I could just think, this was it.

I was astute enough, at least, to recognize that I wasn't simply a victim of what had transpired in Baba's conference room the other day. My mother was right. I HAD asked for this. I had coveted the top job, had dreamt of being made chairperson of my family's powerful company.

So why then was I so miffed when I was given it? I feared it had everything to do with the fact that this was, ultimately, an ill-gotten gain. Baba had chosen me because there had been nobody else. If any of my cousins, or even my fool brother, had made just a wee bit more effort, Baba would have selected them instead. I hadn't won the company because I was better than anyone else; I had won it because they were all rubbish. It was not the same thing.

I had emailed Mrs Bose before my flight had taken off earlier today and told her I would not be in for her 'training session' that day. And that she had to cancel the press conference. And that I was not ready to step into any role, that I would let her and Baba know if and when I was.

That, really, was the crux of the matter here. Baba could give me his company if he wanted to. It didn't mean I had to take it.

I awoke at the crack of dawn feeling, remarkably refreshed. I showered and summoned Ms Friday to let her know I'd like a cup of green tea and a platter of papaya with a squeeze of lime, brought to me at the poolside. I grabbed a notebook and some suntan oil and walked barefoot to the pool. I took one of the white sun loungers under the shade of a vast, lush palm. My breakfast order was there in minutes.

I'd had a good night's sleep, my mind was clear – and now I had to start figuring things out. In a few days, I'd have to go home – back to my domineering grandfather, to the parents who were upset with me, to Bharat, a sort-of boyfriend who I had texted en route to the airport the previous day and whose response I had ignored.

I didn't know what I'd do, but I knew one thing for sure – I wasn't going to consult Jag, my beloved former boyfriend, with whom I'd spoken to just days before Baba's pronouncement. He was dealing with a sick father and had enough on his plate without having to tend to my theatrics. Perhaps the only person I would have loved to have seen right now was Matunga Dada, my loving and kind great-uncle. A few days before Baba had called the meeting that was to change the course of my life, I had seen Dada talking privately in a park with my grandma, Dadi, Baba's wife. The sight of the two of them together had shocked me; I had never seen them in such an intimate moment before. But I was convinced that something was said in that conversation that had compelled Baba to act right away. He had said so himself, right before picking me, that a decision had to be made immediately. That day. Right now, I missed Dada more than anyone; he was my greatest champion and had always been on my side. He would know what to do.

I let the enormous significance of the past couple of days wash over me. This was, indeed, huge. I could imagine myself telling anybody who asked why I was here, alone in this tropical paradise, 'Oh, well, my grandfather left me a billion-dollar conglomerate and I'm not sure what I should do about it. Thoughts, anyone?'

I pulled out my notebook and pen and started scribbling. It was time to make a plan.

Three hours later, I felt positively baked by the sun. I must have turned at least two shades darker. Even though I'd told Ms Friday that I wanted nothing more than to stay alone in my room for the next four days, I was already tiring of my own company. I decided to summon her and have her make an appointment for me at the spa.

At that second, she appeared in front of me.

'Gosh you're good,' I said. 'You just magically showed up. Like a genie.'

Whether she got the joke or not, she smiled. She was holding a phone. 'Miss Badshah, someone is calling for you. His name is Mr Dada. Can I say you are available?'

I jumped up and snatched the phone out of Ms Friday's outstretched hand. My dearest great-uncle must have been thinking of me just as I had been thinking of him.

'Dada?' I said into the phone. 'Let me call you back right away; don't want you spending money on a long-distance call.'

The line crackled. There were voices in the background. He must have been calling me from the ISD booth down the road from his home.

'It's okay, Beta, this will not be a long chat,' he said.

'I'm so glad you called. Something big has happened that I have to tell you about,' I said. Dada would know what to do. Dada always knew what to do.

I noticed now that his voice sounded strange. Remote, somehow. Something was off. Maybe he was sick. Maybe he was calling to give me some bad news. I didn't think I could bear it. Right now I needed my Dada more than I hoped he needed me. Dada always knew what to do.

'Come back,' Dada said, in a strained voice. '... something ... to know...'

'What do you mean, Dada?' I pressed the phone closer to my ear, trying to distinguish his voice over the static on the line. 'Dada?'

His voice was cracking up. '...how hard you worked ... but you can't have...'

The rest of his words cut out.

'What did you say, Dada?' I yelled into the phone.

The line crackled again. Those blasted public phone booths. I vowed to get him a mobile with an unlimited international calling plan.

'...come home ... danger...' were the only words I heard.

'Dada? What!' My voice was rising in panic.

But he was gone.

*To be continued...*

# Acknowledgement

A great many thanks to my publisher, V. K. Karthika at HarperColllins, for shepherding this sequel through to completion, and for the infinite patience required of the process.

I am exceedingly grateful to my editor Ramona Sen – instinctive, insightful and so smart – for seeing what I never might have.

And to Jayne Pillemer in New York, who cast her eye on this three times and was invaluable in helping me shape it.

And lastly, to my longtime agent and friend, Jodie Rhodes, for everything else.